The pilot jockeyed the gunship until Bolan appeared in his sights

Captain Baqir stared in wonderment at the American on the ground, a man without a country, refusing to accept defeat, every inch the awesome human fighting machine the Iranian air-force captain had expected.

For a heartbeat Baqir experienced only sadness as he concentrated on nothing else but the figure who was looking for cover and finding none.

The glory of this kill will take me to the top, the gunship ace thought as his hand snaked inexorably toward the trigger button.

It was a target he could not possibly miss....

MACK BOLAN

The Executioner

DON PENDLETON's EXECUTIONER
MACK BOLAN
Teheran Wipeout

A GOLD EAGLE BOOK FROM
W★RLDWIDE

TORONTO · NEW YORK · LONDON · PARIS
AMSTERDAM · STOCKHOLM · HAMBURG
ATHENS · MILAN · TOKYO · SYDNEY

First edition April 1985

ISBN 0-373-61076-9

Printed in Canada

The problem of *power* is really the fundamental problem of our time and will remain the basic problem of all future history.

—*Herbert Rosinski:* Power and Human Destiny, 1965

No human being should be allowed to play God. Such misguided power only leads to oppression, and deaths, of innocents.

—*Mack Bolan*

In memory of
William Stanford and Charles Hegna
American officials of the
Agency for International Development,
who were slain by Arab hijackers
at Teheran airport, Iran,
in December, 1984.

1

The marksman with the cool eye centered the cross hairs of the sniperscope on his target's forehead.

Mack Bolan ignored the smothering midafternoon heat that baked him atop the flat roof of a five-story building in central Teheran. He had chosen the vantage point carefully, the site affording a clear view of the killing ground a quarter mile away.

The target: Ayatollah Ruholla Khomeini, religious leader of this terrorized hell called the Islamic Republic.

Weapon of the moment was a Weatherby Mark V, a bolt-action .460 Magnum hunting rifle equipped with a twenty-power scope, mounted on a swivel tripod; a big-game weapon with massive stopping power.

And Bolan was hunting big game.

The weapon matched the marksman: Mack Bolan, The Executioner.

And the target centered in the cross hairs was worthy of this executioner.

Bolan wore the nondescript standard attire of the

male Iranian: jeans, shirt and jacket. His silenced 9mm Beretta 93-R nestled in concealed shoulder leather and Big Thunder, Bolan's stainless-steel .44 AutoMag, rode the soldier's right hip on military webbing.

The Executioner studied the image behind the scope's cross hairs. The Ayatollah's pale forehead looked gray under the fierce sun, like the skin of a dead man. Very soon.

Khomeini: a power-mad maniac in the Hitler-Khaddafi-Amin league. But all the more dangerous, Bolan knew, because this slavering barbarian, howling at the gates of civilization was different.

This lunatic fueled himself with irrational religious fervor rather than simple base greed. He was already responsible for the massacre of untold thousands of his country's people, in acts that were pitching Iran into a relentless downward spiral toward the Dark Ages.

The difference was that Khomeini's murderous fanaticism so inflamed his followers that it threatened to suck modern civilization down the tubes to global Armageddon.

Reason enough for an American "combat specialist" named Bolan to risk against-all-odds penetration into the heart of bloody Iran for this one chance at a cannibal without peer. The savage needed stopping, needed killing, real bad before more of the madman's dreams became reality.

Bolan had traveled far and hard to this Teheran

rooftop to do just that in the name of civilization
and for thousands of Iranians. These people badly
needed and deserved a fresh start, Bolan felt, a re-
prieve from an eighty-three-year-old maniac on a
death trip who exploited religion and hatred to
mass hypnotize a country and enforce his own
crazed will.

A man like Bolan, indeed, any rational man of
compassion for his fellow human beings, could
never tolerate such madness as that espoused by the
bearded Ayatollah now in the Executioner's sights.

Most of the world's Muslim population felt
nothing but repugnance for what this crafty old
despot had done to his people. Yet far too many
continued to blindly follow him, much as a good
nation once followed a führer's ravings to its
doom.

Yeah, Iran today is just like that and it wouldn't
stop, Bolan knew, until he squeezed the trigger of
the Weatherby and stopped this Ayatollah.

Khomeini generally made his presence in this
corner of the Mideast felt by portraits of his like-
ness looking down sternly from every available
space, especially in Teheran.

The Ayatollah delivered his occasional addresses, more and more occasional of late accord-
ing to intel reports, in well-guarded indoor sessions
with his cabinet or his mullahs. But today marked
the national celebration of a 1940s Muslim upris-
ing.

To commemorate this auspicious occasion, the Ayatollah had deigned to address thousands of his followers who now packed an open-air pavilion. They were waiting to hear their leader, who, Bolan guessed, would no doubt inflame their frustrations of poverty and lost hope with his monotonic denouncements and proclamations of a *jihad*, the holy war he vowed would turn the Persian Gulf red with the blood of Islam's enemies, including, especially, American blood.

Bolan had reviewed U.S. intel reports theorizing on the Ayatollah's worsening health as evidenced by the recent cutback of personal appearances. Only on special occasions these days did the black-robed, turbaned "holy man" make a showing, such as the present one.

The slavering throng was raucously shouting anti-American slogans until its leader approached the podium and microphone on an elevated stage. Seated behind the speaker's position was a line of the Ayatollah's stern-visaged mullahs and henchmen who conducted a reign of terror over a land that once thought it would find peace and harmony after the revolution toppled the shah.

There had even been vague rumors of the Ayatollah's death, but the boss terror merchant looked healthy enough for a target about to die, thought Bolan in the final heartbeats before he eased back the big Weatherby's trigger.

The Executioner doggedly checked the range

marks of the cross hairs, wiped the sweat from his eyelids and pressed his cheek against the wooden stock.

The moment of the kill was at hand, and Bolan slid his trigger finger back into place.

Like all cannibals who create death and slaughter, Khomeini existed behind a supposedly airtight, invisible shield of security surpassing even that of the President of the United States.

Nearly one thousand plainclothes and uniformed Iranian Revolutionary Guard security men had all of central Teheran sealed tight.

Minutes earlier, two IRG triggermen toting AK-47s and sidearms and stationed on this roof, the tallest building in the vicinity, were wasted with a classic one-two punch when Bolan and Jack Grimaldi had exploded on to the scene with silenced pistols spitting death.

Bolan zapped one man with a brain-coring head shot from the silenced Beretta that chugged no louder than an angry hornet in the afternoon sun.

Grimaldi had squeezed a silenced burst from an Ingram MAC-10 machine pistol that stitched a row of blood-spurting holes across the other IRG goon's chest.

With the roof secured, Grimaldi returned to the street where he now loitered in front of this building. He took up station in a narrow, cobblestone street of small shops that were closed for the Ayatollah's rantings at the nearby pavilion.

Grimaldi stood near an ancient taxi, a rattletrap East European relic purchased from an equally age-worn driver for more rial notes than the decrepit cabbie probably ever saw at one time.

The street fronting the apartment building had enough traffic for Grimaldi's loitering to draw no suspicion, yet most of the neighborhood had interrupted its chores for the Ayatollah's speech and so should be a clear or at least uncluttered withdrawal track.

Bolan had earned the tag Executioner in the Vietnam War where he racked up the highest number of confirmed hits of enemy and civilian targets of any American sniper.

The fact that his compassion for Viet civilians in that conflict earned him the nickname of Sergeant Mercy has always somehow been omitted from media reportage of the man and his deeds during and since that conflict.

Bolan was the personification of the ideal advanced by the Army psychologist who screened and evaluated sniper-team candidates during that war: "A good sniper has to be a man who can kill methodically and unemotionally. Killing in this manner is closely akin to murder in the conscience of many men. What we want is a man who can distinguish between murder and duty, and who can realize that a duty killing is not an act of murder. A man who is also cool and calm when he himself is in jeopardy completes the picture of our sniper ideal."

Bolan had not lately, in his post-Nam campaigns against global evil, brought into use his sniper skills but he saw no other way for this job.

The Ayatollah had to go and Bolan quite simply, quite objectively, saw no one around capable or willing to take on the job except himself. And it mattered not at all to the marksman behind the Weatherby that he operated without the sanction of his or any other government.

Indeed, Bolan's own government had a worldwide Terminate On Sight order on him, issued to all its agents, as did the KGB and most Western powers, a direct result of the Executioner's unsanctioned one-man war against the KGB.

Despite its remarkable success, Bolan's war of attrition rankled those who did not take kindly to a "civilian" treading such classified territory, no matter how successful.

This did not matter to Bolan, either.

The only thing that mattered to Bolan at this moment was squeezing the Weatherby's trigger and canceling out one all-too-powerful cannibal. And yeah, to Bolan it was worth putting everything on the line one more time; worth penetrating this hostile mountainous plateau country of some 636,000 square miles between the Caspian Sea, the world's largest salt-water lake, and the Persian Gulf; more than worth infiltrating into the very heart of the madness.

Teheran.

Founded by the Qajar dynasty, the hillside city nestled six thousand feet above sea level at the base of mighty snowcapped Mount Damavand whose cone shape towered to over eighteen thousand feet from the Elburz Mountains. A once-noble, stately city, Teheran was oppressed under the heel of terror for too damn long to Bolan's way of thinking. Many of Khomeini's own people supported this view, especially those increasing numbers who risked death by forming the People's Mujahedeen, the principal resistance group.

They were the ones responsible for Bolan taking a direct hand in Iranian politics, which had become world politics with the ruling regime's long standing on-again-off-again war with neighboring Iraq. The volatile conflict had escalated to engulf the other Arab states and threatened to force the United States to intervene.

Armageddon, sure. It could come to that.

Washington had plenty of firepower in reserve, including a carrier task force in the Arabian Sea.

American Airborne Warning And Control System—AWACS—surveillance planes monitored four hundred thousand Iranian troops—many of them adolescents and elderly men and women—poised for yet another strike at dug-in Iraqi defenses, waiting for a nod from their Ayatollah for more slaughter to commence.

Bolan had long searched for a handle on the situation there with which to take personal action.

Then the request from the *mujahedeen* reached him.

Khomeini was no figurehead in the modern political sense. The guy was indeed a throwback in that his work, his very will, was the law in this Third World hell.

Western intelligence agencies recognized this. The attempt to free the kidnapped American Embassy personnel from Teheran several years ago had hardly been the last such covert attempt at making things happen there, but all these "official" missions ended in dismal failure.

Bolan knew the odds, yeah, but when this handle came his way he knew the odds did not count, because a time bomb ticked in Iran and this time it would take the world with it unless he could defuse it.

Iran's economy had been devastated by the war with Iraq, oil revenues plunged to only half of what Iran needed to keep the war going and to import basic necessities. Ethnic minorities continued to cause trouble for Khomeini's regime. Nomadic rebels fought in the northwest.

Rebellion of another sort grew in the major cities, spurred by the hideous losses of the war. Army commanders were reluctant to launch a new offensive against well-entrenched Iraq. The army had bogged down, its leadership and a definite rift had begun to appear in the Iranian parliament—the 250-member Majlis. But Iran's ultimate authority gave no sign that he was prepared to abandon his holy war.

Which is why Khomeini's own countrymen had implored Executioner Bolan to lend his expertise to the problem, giving this coolheaded "duty killer" exactly the handle he needed.

He squeezed into the trigger pull.

The roar of the big-game Weatherby shattered the broiling afternoon air.

And through the sniperscope, the Executioner saw the distant head of Ayatollah Khomeini explode like the gut of a dead animal left in the sun too long.

2

Bolan got the hell off that roof and toward the street fast as he could.

He reluctantly left behind the Weatherby. Earlier, when Grimaldi had parked the car in front of the building and Bolan brought the rifle up to the roof, the big weapon had been wrapped in cloth, carried like anything from curtain rods to a long pipe. But that had been minutes ago on a routine weekday afternoon except for the nearby rally.

The Weatherby's report would have been heard by everyone in the vicinity.

Bolan registered a quick impression of Iranian security men on nearby lower rooftops swiveling around, but none of them could pinpoint the source of the shot, though it would not take them long.

It would take Bolan long enough to reach Grimaldi and the taxi and for them to get away; too long if he emerged from the building toting anything that remotely resembled a rifle so soon after the kill.

He sidestepped the two dead men sprawled near the roof door and pulled it shut behind him. He hustled down the inside narrow stairway.

He negotiated the sharp turns, picking up speed, passing deserted dimly lighted corridors that stank of too many people crammed too close together. He also discerned the smell of fear.

He would have preferred taking out the whole row of the boss cannibal's cabinet who shared the stage with Khomeini, but the seconds wasted on such a whim could buy a safe withdrawal.

The Iranian freedom underground unit that had requested the Executioner to carry out this "impossible hit" figured termination of Khomeini would do it. They and Bolan envisioned a more or less bloodless coup after this, wherein cooler heads in Teheran close to the top could steer this ravaged country back on the track to rejoin the twentieth century.

He slowed his pace when he reached the bottom step. He approached the fly-specked half-glass front door of a narrow foyer.

The world would be going topsy-turvey a quarter mile away at the open-air pavilion, a crowd out of control. Bolan knew that before the blistering sun set this day Teheran would be sealed tighter than a drum.

Grimaldi had worked with Bolan as backup on missions for years. The Vietnam-vet pilot ace with the Italian-movie-star visage and happy-go-lucky style had as much skill behind the wheel of a car, any car, as he had in the cockpit of any warplane.

Bolan grasped the door handle, then he saw the trouble.

The ancient taxi was idling at the curb in front of the apartment-house door, Grimaldi behind the wheel.

A uniformed Teheran policeman was leaning over the driver's side window in heated conversation with Grimaldi.

Bolan eased the door inward and stepped from the building onto the front step with a natural, casual move.

He scanned the narrow cobblestone street, encompassing in a glance all that might lurk there as he closed the door behind him.

Word about the assassination had not had time to reverberate this far. It would within another minute or two. The few pedestrians down there had heard the shot, but gunfire is common throughout Iran. Nobody seemed concerned.

The policeman saw Bolan emerge from the building. The cop straightened and shifted his attention from Grimaldi.

Bolan casually made his way down the steps toward the cab.

The officer snarled something at Bolan in Farsi, and Bolan wondered if he would have to kill this man.

The cop waved an irritated "the hell with it, get

out of here" gesture at both the "cabbie" and the "fare," then turned and began to move away.

Bolan started to slide into the front seat of the cab.

A sedan with official markings careered, fishtailing, screeching, burning rubber into this cross street from half a block away. The vehicle straightened out from the turn and rocketed toward the cab, and the policeman, who had not gone very far, paused in his progress away from the taxi to turn and investigate the commotion.

Grimaldi popped the car into a forward lurch the moment Bolan made it into the front seat alongside him. The momentum slammed the door shut after Bolan and the taxi shot away from the curb, its aged engine straining.

Bolan unleathered Big Thunder.

"U-turn us out of here, Jack."

The numbers had run out, but all the while Bolan felt something nagging at him. Something more than a beat cop trying to shake down a cabbie over some minor traffic infraction, something more, even, than a racing sedan full of IRG security hardmen. Bolan felt sure of it in his gut.

Something had gone wrong with the hit on the roof. And he could not identify it.

Grimaldi palmed the wheel.

The squeal of tires on cobblestone again filled the air, bounding from wall to wall of the narrow street. Grimaldi swung the car around without slackening speed.

The government sedan roared closer, the confrontation escalating to flash point.

The Teheran cop grabbed for a holstered sidearm.

Pedestrians scurried for safety in the sunlight.

The taxi clambered on and off the opposite curb, Grimaldi played the steering wheel and gears with controlled urgency.

"The Ayatollah?" he inquired.

"Mission accomplished," Bolan grunted. "I think."

Gunfire peppered the cab's exterior from the pursuing sedan no more than a car length behind and gaining.

Bolan straight-armed a death round from the .44 AutoMag at the chase vehicle.

Three weapons were already sticking out of its windows like antennae, and the Executioner was not surprised at the security reflex to the rooftop report of the Weatherby. Word of the assassination must have been relayed over two-way radio, the first wave of the net beginning to tighten around the city.

The AutoMag's 240-grain slug punched through the sedan's windshield, and the driver's head exploded all over his partners.

The sedan weaved crazily for a moment, then climbed the curb to pile full speed into a brick wall. Bolan heard the wrenching impact of flattening metal and shattering glass and knew the other three in the car could never survive a crash like that.

The shrill sounds of a policeman's whistle pierced the air.

Grimaldi pegged off a burst from his Ingram MAC-10 that punched the whistle back into the cop's mouth. The dead man stumbled back and collapsed into the wreckage of the sedan.

Grimaldi powered the taxi for everything it had toward the nearest intersection.

The taxi's engine filled the interior of the car with its whine as they rocketed away from there.

"I should've blown away that cop when he tried to shake me down," Grimaldi growled, downshifting. "A real small-time sharpie, he thought."

Bolan braced himself for the coming turn.

"Head us west, Jack."

"You got it."

The cab took the turn on two squealing tires.

Grimaldi straightened out the fishtailing car, standing on the gas pedal and upshifting.

Bolan eyed their backtrack, his finger curled around Big Thunder's trigger.

An armored personnel carrier bulleted from a side street up ahead to stop across the width of the street, blocking the cab.

"Damn," Grimaldi grunted under his breath.

The troop truck sported six Iranian-army storm troopers in crisp khakí uniforms, toting rifles, with two more rifle-armed men in the cab.

The soldiers saw the oncoming taxi and commenced debarking snappily from the truck.

Grimaldi pumped the taxi's brakes.

The cab's speed dropped to forty mph, enough to slow down, not enough to avoid impact.

"Out," growled Bolan.

He and Grimaldi shouldered their doors and toppled in rolls from the taxi a couple of seconds before the cab ate up the distance to smash into the side of the armored vehicle.

The trooper climbing down from the side of the truck's cab had no time to leap away, and the oncoming car crushed him like a bug.

The impact tilted the truck onto its side, flinging men amid shouts of pain that ended abruptly when the unlucky ones slammed against pavement and wall of a nearby building.

The other soldiers recovered their composure enough to track weapons at the two Americans who now came out of their rolls to regain combat crouches at either side of the street.

Bolan hammered off three rounds from Big Thunder, and a trio of Khomeini enforcers got their life forces splashed across the truck behind them before toppling dead.

Grimaldi assumed a two-handed shooting stance.

The Ingram bucked in his hand.

The driver of the truck was reaching for the dash microphone when he caught some .45 slugs in the chest and through the throat. The fusillade pitched him backward out of the cab with the mike, torn from its cord, in his hand.

The few surviving soldiers scrambled for cover.

Bolan glanced along their backtrack.

Another troop carrier appeared at the far end of the street, blocking that avenue of withdrawal.

More soldiers poured from that truck and began advancing cautiously.

The two Americans withdrew on the run down a cobblestone alley not wide enough for a vehicle. They reached cover of the alley walls at the instant soldiers from both personnel carriers opened fire with automatic weapons.

The air whined with the piercing whistle of bullets and ricochets, then the salvo stopped, leaving a ringing silence in its wake.

Bolan knew the soldiers would be charging after them in hot pursuit.

Bolan and Grimaldi covered the distance to a junction in the alley ahead in long, fast strides.

"We split up?" Grimaldi asked.

"Negative."

They had but a yard to go when half a dozen Iranian civilians erupted from the blind side of the alley intersection.

The civilians lifted their voices in shouts to alert the soldiers that they had cornered the Americans.

The six unarmed civilians closed in on Bolan and Grimaldi, obviously expecting the foreigners to follow the sensible course and surrender.

Grimaldi pulled up his pistol.

Bolan waved the gun down.

"Spare 'em, Jack."

Bolan felt no fight against unarmed men who thought themselves good citizens. He sailed into the cluster of robed locals with a flurry of martial-arts kicks and punches delivered at blinding speed.

Within seconds four of the civilians toppled sideways like bowling pins.

Grimaldi moved in and took out the final two with sharp blows from the butt of his pistol.

The Americans moved past the civilians and rounded the corner of the *T*.

The other end of the alley was filled with Iranian uniforms, bright in the brassy sunshine, advancing on the run from both ends of the street. Bolan and Grimaldi rounded the corner an instant before the soldiers opened fire with another salvo of jackhammering autofire.

The confines of the alley echoed with shouts and bootfalls of the rushing soldiers closing in.

Blank stone walls of two-level buildings stared back at Bolan and Grimaldi from either end of the *T* in the alleyway.

No escape.

Boxed in.

They crossed to the far wall. They turned, backs to the wall to make a stand, Grimaldi palming a fresh magazine into his Ingram, Bolan with a reloaded Big Thunder in one fist, the Beretta in the other.

His survival instincts flared for some way, any way, out of this.

The walls were too high to scale to the roof of any of the buildings.

From around the corner of the *T* they heard panicky shouts, then rapid-fire bursts from AK-47s. The shouting stopped.

The advancing IRG storm troopers had not spared the civilians as Bolan had.

Shouts of bloodlust filled the air.

The first wave of men poured into the juncture of the *T*, AKs glinting in the harsh sun.

The soldiers spotted Bolan and Grimaldi instantly.

"Aw, *shit*," Grimaldi said with feeling.

3

Two things happened at once.

The first five soldiers to spill around the corner of the alley tracked their assault rifles up for the kill at the exact instant Bolan and Grimaldi picked their targets.

And a rope ladder dropped from the roof of a building that formed one side of the boxed-in killground.

Bolan triggered Beretta and AutoMag. The 93-R chugged on silenced auto, popping 9mm zingers. Big Thunder boomed, deafening reports swallowing the grunts of the dying as .44 and 9mm sureshots took lives.

Two terrorists of the state toppled back, dead on their feet, khaki uniforms spurting red.

The soldier next to them caught a head shot and so did the next guy.

The fifth Khomeini enforcer started to turn for cover. Grimaldi stopped him in his tracks with a .45-caliber sizzler that cored the guy in one ear and out the other.

Bolan risked a glance at the roof.

A woman, a good-looking blonde he did not recognize, had completed fastening hooks at one end of the rope ladder to the edge of the roof. She gestured to the men, nervously but not frantic.

Nervy, thought Bolan.

"Hurry," she called in English, glancing at the junction of the alley where bodies lay and gun smoke swirled.

She crouched low on the roof, her pleated summer skirt and blouse making her look like a million bucks, Bolan noted. The lady clasped a shoulder bag close to her side, and from it she tugged a small Walther PPK.

Two IRG goons risked glances around the corner of the alley, their AKs poking with them.

Bolan hammered off two thunderclaps from Big Thunder and both those heads evaporated into bursting red mist.

"Up the ladder," Bolan instructed Grimaldi from a crouch, combat eyes and both pistols on the *T*. "I'll cover you."

"Man, I'd follow that blonde anywhere," Grimaldi said with a chuckle.

The Italian jumped to catch the fourth rope rung of the ladder and continued up the side of the wall like a scrambling spider.

Bolan holstered the Beretta and hustled after Grimaldi, grabbing the rung with his left hand for leverage, the right hand still fisting the .44 hand cannon. He made it halfway up when someone barked orders in a language he did not understand. Then an officer and six reluctant Iranian Revolutionary Guard soldiers stormed around the corner of the alley, automatic fire blazing from AK-47s.

At targets that had disappeared.

A volley of autofire riddled the wall where Bolan and Grimaldi had stood less than five seconds before, ricocheting harmlessly in all directions.

The confused soldiers ceased firing and swiveled eyes and rifles upward, sighting Bolan as he reached his free hand up the edge of the roof, his legs supported by the rope ladder.

He twisted around from his position and triggered off a recoil-heavy sound from Big Thunder that reverberated in the boxed death ground, pitching a trooper into a lifeless sprawl.

Grimaldi and the million-dollar blonde triggered off several rounds each from the roof as Bolan swung the AutoMag back from its recoil buck to take out another IRG gunner.

The soldiers below caught incoming rounds that slammed them back into the wall. Their comrades remained out of sight.

Bolan hauled himself onto the roof with one final acrobatic swing, then paused to replace the spent clip in Big Thunder.

Grimaldi used the moment to reload his Ingram.

Miss Million Bucks tugged up the rope ladder after them.

Bolan spared her an iced glance.

"I suppose you have a car nearby, too," he said wryly.

She gathered up the rope ladder in a bundle, moving with grace and speed. Her lovely strong legs and well-curved thighs provided the American fighting duo with a nice sight in the eye blink when her skirt hiked upward as she moved.

"In the street, two buildings down."

She hurried away from the two men.

Bolan and Grimaldi joined her in the short leap to the next building, the trio continuing across that roof.

Behind them in the distance they heard the rabble of soldiers in the alley, arguing about the boxed-in targets who seemed to vanish like dissipating smoke.

The sun in the white sky blazed down upon three figures hustling across rooftops.

Every dog in the neighborhood was barking and yowling along with the engine sounds and shouts of excitement as word of the assassination of Ayatollah Khomeini spread through the city.

The roofs along this section of Teheran had been cleared of security and troops in the five minutes or less since the hit, the forces mobilizing on the streets.

The two men and the blonde leaped across a second narrow space to another building, the woman heading straight for a doorway set into the roof.

Bolan made the door first, then motioned Grimaldi away from the door.

The woman stepped aside, and Bolan could feel her wide brown eyes appraising him.

He held the AutoMag up, ready for anything, unlatched the door with his left hand and stepped well aside from it and the line of possible fire from within. He nudged the door farther open with a toe.

No gunfire.

He peered into the dimness of a stairway every bit as deserted as that of the apartment building he had fired from. This residential structure had two levels. He could see down to the foyer that faced a street adjacent to the one where the IRG foot soldiers thought they had the Americans cornered.

"Where is your car?" Bolan asked the woman.

"In front of this building."

Wailing sirens carried from the direction of the pavilion.

No one had yet appeared on any of the surrounding rooftops to give chase or indicate that this route of escape had been detected.

Bolan gambled one more second for a final scrutiny of the mystery lady appraising him. He saw no other options.

"Okay, miss. Lead the way."

She did.

Bolan followed, careful eyes probing ahead of them over her shoulder as they hurried down the stairs, Big Thunder ready to unleash at the first sight of trouble or a trap.

Grimaldi eased the roof door shut after them and brought up the rear.

Midway down the second-floor corridor, a door eased inward as they made the landing.

Wide-eyed children peered out curiously for a second, then the little innocents disappeared with a yank from unseen parents and the door slammed shut.

When Bolan and the blonde reached the bottom step and the foyer, the woman started straight toward the street door.

Bolan halted her with the AutoMag, the .44 nudging her shoulder as he edged her aside.

Grimaldi reached the bottom step.

As they crowded into the foyer, Bolan again exercised caution in inching open the door for a scan of the street.

An idling Mercedes was parked at the curb, its chrome reflecting the fierce sunlight.

A man Bolan did not recognize sat behind the steering wheel.

Bolan saw a side street empty of any pedestrians. He figured that the neighborhood had either gravitated toward the sounds of shooting and activity in the next block from where Bolan and his companions had escaped, or had sought refuge from more killing.

He heard the heavy rumble of an approaching

vehicle. He eased the door shut, leaving only a tiny crack through which he eyeballed another lumbering armored troop carrier. It rounded the corner and chugged past.

The truck turned at the next corner on its way to reinforce the soldiers one block over, leaving behind a street rank with diesel fumes but still empty.

"Now," Bolan instructed.

They broke from the entranceway, Grimaldi and Bolan occasionally turning around to cover their track.

The blonde started toward the front passenger side of the car.

"Uh-uh." Bolan stopped her with the ice in his voice. "Ride in back with my friend, please."

Grimaldi opened the back door of the car and held it open for her.

The blonde's eyes flared with anger as she glanced at Bolan. She started to say something, then a stutter of automatic-weapon fire crackled from the next block. The woman followed Bolan's suggestion.

Grimaldi popped into the back seat.

Bolan hotfooted around the rear of the vehicle to tug open the door on the driver's side.

The driver opened his mouth to protest, then read the determined visage of the man behind the AutoMag.

The driver slid over.

Bolan executed a sharp U-turn that avoided the

curb, but instead of flooring the gas pedal to get them the hell out of there, he tooled away at a sedate speed in the opposite direction from the activity.

The ex-driver cleared his throat.

"Ah, say, bud...maybe we oughta feed her some gas, huh?"

Two unmarked sedans full of rifle toters careered around the corner up ahead and raced past the Mercedes. More Iranian Revolutionary Guard security "closing the net," Bolan guessed.

The government cars sped by, sirens whining, their occupants sparing hardly a glance at the unhurried pace of the Mercedes.

The blonde beside Grimaldi in the back seat chuckled, an unexpected, pleasant sound.

"Let the man drive, Chuck," she advised her male companion. "This one knows how to handle himself, don't you, big guy?"

Bolan concentrated on his driving, his right fist filled with the AutoMag, index finger curled around the trigger, reviewing the events of the last few minutes: the pullout, the two unknowns in the Mercedes with him and Jack and the activity around the car.

Another armored truck barreling into the fray sped past.

"Smart," Grimaldi said, grinning. "Who'd figure we'd head toward the pavilion?"

Grimaldi kept his Ingram MAC-10 drawn in his

right fist. He used his left to pull out a battered pack of cigarettes from his hip pocket. He offered the blonde a smoke with the legendary Grimaldi style intact.

"Guess it's time for introductions, gorgeous. Funny place to run into Americans."

The cool blonde did not miss a beat. She reached for the smoke and fired it and his with her own lighter.

"I was about to make the same observation," she said, smiling while she exhaled smoke.

The man in the passenger seat dabbed a handkerchief across his damp brow. Bolan estimated him to be in his midthirties, noting his average build and appearance. He wore lightweight whites and a jittery demeanor.

"Ah, I could give you directions—"

Bolan steered the Mercedes onto a wide thoroughfare bordered by trees and long brownstone walks, continuing on the track away from the pavilion and the concentration of activity.

Traffic on this street seemed sluggish under the oppressive heat; no outward indications that the dragnet had reached this far.

The occasional pedestrians were traditionally garbed, veiled women on their way to or from some nearby market who registered no interest at the passing symbol of wealth on wheels as the Mercedes continued along, picking up speed.

Bolan glanced at his watch. Eleven minutes had

elapsed since the assassination of the Ayatollah Khomeini. Eleven minutes.

Bolan's uneasiness about the mission gnawed some more at his gut.

"Let's have some names, you two."

"That's not acting very appreciative after all we just did for you," the blonde piped up from the back seat. "I'd say we saved your lives back there."

Grimaldi finished his smoke and snubbed it out in the ashtray.

"I guess my buddy and I are sort of wondering about that too, sweetheart."

The man next to Bolan pocketed his handkerchief.

"Hey, when we saw you guys in trouble—"

"Names," Bolan repeated.

The guy gulped audibly.

"Ah, yeah, okay. . . Chuck Talbot is my handle. This is my wife, Ellie."

Ellie spoke up from the back.

"Those soldiers wanted you guys real bad. How about that?"

Chuck appeared not to notice her question.

"Turn right at this corner," he told Bolan. "Our place is the second entranceway on the right."

Bolan made the turn.

None of this played right, and that's why he had no choice but to see what these two had in mind.

"Whoever you guys are, you can stay with us until it's dark," Ellie offered. "Then I guess you'll want to leave, right? Neither of you looks like a couple hundred night patrols would stop you, do they, Chuck?"

She had a candid style, not too brassy but ballsy enough, and Bolan liked her.

He hoped she would not die tonight.

The narrow side street onto which Bolan steered the Mercedes had a shaded exclusiveness about it, the incredible afternoon sun shielded by evenly planted oleanders that met overhead; a street lined with private villas behind ten-foot-high walls.

The heat and sweat and dying could have been a thousand miles away, Bolan reflected. He steered the Mercedes through a break in the wall.

A crushed-limestone driveway circled around a fountain that burbled merrily in front of a two-level Mediterranean-style residence, the grounds shaded by more oleander and date palms. The walls assured complete privacy.

Bolan braked the car and switched off the ignition beneath a carport at the front entrance of the home.

Talbot cleared his throat.

"Ah, maybe some tall cool drinks would loosen everybody up, huh? Come on in. It's a sort of temporary abode, you might say, but we stocked her up with all the comforts of home, if you know what I mean, right, Ellie?"

Ellie did not answer.

Bolan studied the house. He knew Grimaldi would have Talbot covered with the Ingram from the back seat.

"Anyone in there waiting for us?" he asked Talbot.

The American appeared more relaxed.

"Nope, just me and Ellie, and it's about time we had some homegrown company, if you know what I mean."

Ellie made an unladylike snort that could have meant anything, opened her door and started from the car.

"So what are we waiting for, gentlemen? Dodging bullets makes me thirsty."

They alighted from the car and entered the house and only towering Mount Damavand saw them.

The roomy, high-ceilinged interior had a chilly, aseptic, unlived-in look, thought Bolan. He followed the three inside and shut the front door behind him, Big Thunder still in his right fist.

"This way, gang," Talbot beckoned cheerily from where he headed the small group.

Talbot stepped sprightly through a doorway off the right of the entrance foyer, Ellie following her husband.

Grimaldi, behind Ellie, glanced at Bolan, his MAC-10 unholstered.

Bolan nodded and Grimaldi returned the nod

and went on in, striking up his standard easygoing patter to the husband and wife.

"Quite a place, yeah, quite a place. Didn't know they treated Americans so good over here."

Bolan noted another archway leading to a living room and dining room opposite this den-type room. He detected no signs of habitation about the house; no magazines, no personal belongings in sight anywhere.

"Sort of ungentlemanly," Grimaldi continued to Talbot, "letting your better half climb that roof while you sat in the car, I mean, don't cha think, sport?"

Bolan stepped last into the den, which was dominated by a well-stocked liquor cabinet by the far wall.

Ellie answered Grimaldi without hesitation.

"I'm the one who suggested I go up to that roof. I thought it would go better if one of their soldiers stopped me. This is not a liberated country, you know. Sexually, I mean. They would not have searched a woman; they would not imagine a woman could be involved."

Bolan positioned himself with his back near a wall that afforded him full view of the room and entrance and a portion of the hallway outside the door.

Grimaldi took a similar position across the room.

"And what are you involved in?" asked Bolan. "I want to hear it all. Now."

The blonde avoided Bolan's icy gaze. She deferred to her husband for the first time.

Talbot paused at an end table beside a couch and opened a cigarette case, took one out, tapped and lighted it. He looked like a man considering several replies, settling on the most direct.

"Why, I'm an arms dealer, old buddies, or hadn't you guessed? I've always preferred 'gun-runner,' actually. A little more romantic, if you know what I mean." He turned his back to them and started to the liquor cabinet. "Now, what will it be, gentlemen?"

"The truth," Bolan growled. "If you know what I mean."

Talbot turned very, very slowly to stare across the room at the wide muzzle of the long-barreled stainless-steel hand cannon extended from Bolan's straight-armed aim.

Talbot chuckled without conviction.

"Hey, dude...ah, what's the idea? The only reason I'm even confiding in you at all is...them soldiers chasing you and all. I mean, you guys aren't exactly on the up and up yourselves, if you know what I...ah, are you? Maybe we can do some business?"

"I'll explain this to you just once," Bolan growled, his arm unwavering, AutoMag trained between Talbot's eyes. "You could be arms dealers and that could explain why two citizens of the most hated nation in Iran get VIP treatment and a cabinet full of liquor that is strictly forbidden in this country, but it won't explain what put the lady here on that roof at the exact moment we needed help the most."

Grimaldi, his Ingram at his side, watched Mrs. Talbot closely.

"With a rope ladder, yet."

The blonde's chuckle sounded like rocks in a glass in the brittle silence. She regarded Chuck.

"It appears our guests have been underestimated by our superiors. I knew this was a foolish plan."

The man at the bar sighed resignedly and seemed to relax. He stared unblinking into the wide-bored AutoMag.

"I am Major Yuri Steranko of the KGB," he told Bolan. He nodded to the blonde. "This is my assistant, Tanya Yesilov."

The lady moved with a dancer's grace to stand between Bolan and her "husband."

She stared into the AutoMag's muzzle and into the eyes of the gunman behind it.

"And what will you do now, Mack Bolan? Execute us?"

4

KGB: The Komitet Gosudarstvennoi Bezopasnosti; the Soviet Union's Committee for State Security.

More dangerous than the Mafia had ever been because these gangsters mask their lust for power beneath a network Bolan recognized as the most sophisticated terrorist apparatus in history.

Bolan held a most personal blood debt against the KGB.

Until recently, Bolan had commanded a covert, White House-sanctioned antiterrorist force that operated worldwide to curb a terrorist tide that threatened to drown the civilized countries of the world in a very uncivilized bloodbath.

Bolan's twenty-plus successful missions aimed at thwarting this orchestrated menace to the Free World impressed upon him that world terrorism in fact was a simmering volcano.

In fact it burned red-hot with nothing less than world exploitation, a goal that grew ever closer to becoming reality. A realization struck home tragically when the "volcano" itself—the KGB—staged an almost successful commando raid on

Bolan's base, Stony Man Farm, in rural Virginia near America's capital.

The KGB-organized assault team was repelled, but the cost to the Stony Man operation and to Bolan himself was staggering. Good people, good friends in Bolan's fight, died during the attack, including April Rose, the Farm's projects coordinator and the woman Bolan had loved and still did.

Bolan could never conceive of a soul such as April's, that had lived so large, as ever being dead. She lived in the heart of this soldier and would forever.

In a way Bolan felt that this war of his, against an evil so widespread it would confound the average person, had nothing to do with anything like revenge. But deep inside, with all efforts to rationalize his motivations aside, the big warrior knew that just a small part of what he did may have been motivated by that savage emotion.

Bolan, however, was hardly average by any stretch of the imagination.

The U.S. Army had trained this fighting man well, both in the jungles of Nam and during his antiterrorist wars.

The aftermath of the Stony Man Farm attack had seen the Executioner unmask a KGB spy planted at White House level. For Bolan there was no other course but to terminate the sleazeball who had pulled the strings resulting in the attack and April's death. And after that he had seen no alternative but to pursue this spreading cancer, this KGB.

Enough good people had already tried that, sure, but America's espionage apparatus has never recovered from the misuses of the Nixon years.

The CIA, the FBI, the NSA and all the rest had their operations brought into the light for all to study, including the cannibals in the Kremlin. These people talked "arms limitations" and the like when it suited them while they subjugated more and more of the world map for their dreamed-of world slave state.

These Soviet terrormongers guffawed up their sleeves at how stupid America continued to dig its own grave.

The Russian agent uncovered and executed by Bolan in the White House had meant to chip away from within at what little effectiveness remained.

Bolan terminated the guy and declared his intention to take on the KGB with or without official sanction.

He had realized since Vietnam that the meek would never inherit a savage earth; in fact, they were losing it inch by inch to the savages of the Mafia, of the Kremlin and of the terrorist networks who had no use at all for laws except to turn them on victims afraid to back up their laws.

Power, money and grab for both is the name of the cannibal's game, taking whatever he wants from anyone not strong enough to fight back, be it a defenseless nation or a defenseless elderly woman on an inner-city street.

Bolan drew no distinction between terrorists, KGB and the Mafia, except the terrorist and KGB hoods had the savvy to cloak their acts behind smoke screens of rhetoric.

The Executioner knew that anyone who didn't think the savages were winning need only compare the world map of today with one of thirty years ago. The contrast was stark and there for all to see.

Only a blind man or someone with nefarious intentions could not discern the threatening magnitude of what fired Mack Bolan's soul to undertake this most dangerous mile of a dangerous life: democracies, governments of the people, disappearing with alarming, increased regularity.

The soldier well understood that it would not be long before the cancer began eating at America's borders from the south. No one disagreed with this; it is fact. Bolan had seen the process with his own eyes in enough hellgrounds around the world to know, but a powerful government hog-tied by popularity-poll politicians and intimidated by the myth of "world opinion" seemed helpless to do anything about it.

And this is why Executioner Bolan saw no other course of action than the one he took: the very *un*sanctioned private war that had earned him

Priority Number One on the Terminate On Sight lists of Communist and Western spy agencies, including the KGB and its seven hundred thousand agents worldwide.

Bolan's one-man war was called crazy by almost everyone.

Combat specialist Bolan, however, and the few like Grimaldi with whom he remained in contact, knew far better.

Bolan had fought some "crazy" wars before, first against the cannibalism of communism in Vietnam, then in another "crazy" one-man war against the Mafia that had brought that behemoth of savagery to its knees; then against world terrorism, whose network he had crippled beyond repair or reunification with the help of his Stony Man Team and his government-sponsored combat units, Phoenix Force and Able Team.

April was gone now.

Dammit.

And the ones responsible would pay.

Not for revenge, uh-uh.

Bolan had spent enough time in Russia, had met and befriended enough good people in that sprawling gulag, for him not to mistake the power mongers in the Kremlin for the citizens under their heel in Russia and elsewhere. Nor did he mistake the KGB as merely the "sword and shield of the Soviet Union" as one Kremlin boss went on record as labeling it.

The KGB's activities in the name of socialist expansionism were as capitalistic as could be; billions a year, extorted from Soviet-occupied and satellite countries, funneling through a Mafialike pyramid setup into the Swiss bank accounts of a select few boss savages who would feel right at home in any Mafia boardroom.

No damn difference at all.

And if no one else was willing, soldier Bolan saw it as his duty to turn away from his government and take on the unbelievably impossible odds.

Seven hundred thousand to one.

Some odds, yeah.

It was a war Bolan knew he would not, could not win.

Not with his own government against him.

But a good soldier does not shirk his duty, and Bolan would continue this war of attrition. He would cut that seven hundred thousand down some.

Not for revenge, no.

This Executioner waged his war everlasting because he valued life. He was raised with the American ideals of peacefulness and respect of human life implanted in him from as far back as he could remember, and he still valued those ideals.

He was a gentle man who lived in a not so gentle world. The continual inner conflict of this warrior's soul was that he was an aware man with a reverence for life, and yet his own existence was turbulent and his war everlasting because of that reverence. But however distasteful in the eyes of civilized man, or, indeed, his own eyes, by God, Bolan would carry on.

Grandiose justification for wholesale slaughter, his critics called it from their safe, cozy sidelines well back from where the Executioner waded through rivers of blood. He was the one who trod the front lines to keep those critics safe from a savage world beyond the artificial existence they lived in.

This Executioner, living a sentence of death, walked his last bloody mile on earth doing what must be done; not exultantly but regretfully.

To believe in something is one thing, Bolan knew; to be willing to die for something is the true measure of commitment and a life lived large to the last heartbeat.

This Executioner knew no other way.

He attacked evil wherever he felt his presence could be beneficial, not limiting his operations to the KGB exclusively, his war taking him to every corner of the world since breaking away from government sanction; from the jungles of Cambodia to the plains of Kansas.

Bolan financed his operations with a "war chest" appropriated from the cannibals whose operations he destroyed. The few well-hidden links to his past, intel sources like Hal Brognola,

Stony Man Farm's White House liaison, and "Bear" Kurtzman, the Farm's computer whiz, forever wheelchair-ridden by enemy fire the night of the attack that took April, aided and abetted Bolan's wildcat missions.

Bear continued to oversee operations at the Farm, which continued despite Bolan's hitting into the cold on his own.

Brognola remained as White House liaison.

And Grimaldi, ever the ace in the hole, like right now in Teheran.

Bolan knew, though, that for the most part, the hardest part, this bloody last mile, could only be his own and he would have it no other way.

And now Blood Road had brought him to Hell Town itself.

Bloody Teheran.

And the KGB, again, where Bolan had not expected them.

This Executioner expected and anticipated only one certainty at this point.

Teheran would get bloodier before Bolan finished with it.

5

"Whether or not I terminate you two here and now depends on what you have to say," Bolan told Tanya Yesilov.

He lowered Big Thunder slightly so the muzzle was not pointing between the blond lovely's clear brown eyes.

Grimaldi held his Ingram aimed at Yuri Steranko.

The atmosphere in the den pulsed with tension.

Steranko stepped next to the woman who claimed to be his wife. She stood facing the Executioner.

Steranko ignored the sweat beads along his hairline. The man who had called himself "Chuck Talbot" stared at the guy with the AutoMag, trying to discern something indiscernible in eyes like blue chips of death.

"We are mortal enemies, you and us." Steranko spoke quietly. "Why should Mack Bolan, the Executioner, spare the lives of two agents of the KGB?"

Grimaldi clucked his tongue.

"You sound real anxious to die, comrade."

"I am a realist. I would appreciate an answer."

"I'll take the answers," Bolan growled. "No more dodges. Talk, one or both of you. If you know anything about me, you know I don't bluff. Do yourselves a favor and believe I'm not bluffing now."

"I think, Yuri," the blonde purred, "that to co-operate with these gentlemen at this juncture would be in keeping with our orders." She studied Bolan. "I did not toss that rope ladder to you a short while ago simply so that you could put a bullet in my head, dear sir."

"Start with that, then. You know who I am. You were in the right place at the right time. You know why I came to Teheran?"

Tanya nodded.

"You came to kill someone who needs killing. Our orders were and remain to monitor your activities."

"You didn't trail us to that rooftop. I'd have spotted a pair like you. You knew I'd be there."

"An informer," Grimaldi grunted.

Steranko cleared his throat.

"You will not kill us until you know the name of our informant. That is our insurance, is it not?"

"Khomeini hates the Russians as much as he hates good old America," Grimaldi went on. "Hell, he executed most of the Communist party here a few months back."

"It was the hope of our superiors that, Iran being the only, er, spot on the globe right now where U.S. and Soviet interests coincide," Steranko replied in unaccented American, "that in the matter of eliminating Khomeini, we, that is, our organization, might benefit from your own actions here."

"You could try," Bolan grunted. "The American impersonations are great, by the way, and the arms-dealer cover takes off heat for a while, but why risk it?"

"Can you not guess?"

"You've got your own play. The army?"

Steranko's nod and tight smile confirmed an easy guess.

"May I smoke?"

Bolan holstered Big Thunder. Give them enough rope, he decided. His fingertips lingered near the holstered hawgleg.

"Why don't we all smoke. Jack, position yourself outside. Recon what you can of the neighborhood."

"Check," Grimaldi said and left the room.

Bolan brought out his own pack of smokes and fired one.

The Russians sat side by side on the couch.

Bolan perched on a stool facing them, the door and hallway behind the man and woman.

"Whose house is this?"

"It belongs to a General Mahmoud," said Steranko. "The general has granted permission for us to use it in the event of an emergency."

"Which I would say this afternoon most certainly was," the lady finished for her "husband."

At that instant Steranko sprang from the couch, gripping a pistol. It looked to Bolan like a Walther PPK, the diminutive handgun yanked from a hiding place beneath the cushions on the couch, put there long ago for a contingency such as this.

Steranko blurred into action, the Walther tracking speed-draw fast by a guy who had appeared so flustered. Another good impersonation, thought Bolan as he unleathered the silenced Beretta from its shoulder holster in a lightning cross draw, faster than Steranko could ever hope to be.

In the sudden realization that he had lost, Steranko's eyes widened into almost comic circles, just like his mouth, which now tried to cry out something to the Executioner, who had been ready for something like this since they had walked into the den.

The discreet, low cough of the Beretta punched a silenced 9mm projectile into Yuri Steranko's mouth, stuffing any last words back into the guy's brains, as pieces of skull exploded from the back of the cannibal's head.

The Russian toppled onto the couch, spewing rivulets of blood, then rolled forward when the couch stopped his dead-fall. His corpse collapsed into a fetal position between Bolan and the woman, who melded into the far end of the couch.

The blonde did not appear shocked. She stood, averting her eyes from the deceased "husband."

Bolan also stood, tracking the Beretta to the heart region beneath Tanya Yesilov's shapely left breast.

"I think now would be a good time to toss over your hardware, too."

She carefully withdrew her Walther PPK from her handbag, fingertips clasping the pistol by its stubby barrel.

Bolan watched her every movement. He reached down to pick up Steranko's pistol, which lay near the man's outstretched right hand. Bolan dropped the pistol into a jacket pocket.

Tanya tossed her gun to Bolan, staring at him as if transfixed, more speculative than before.

"You knew?" she asked tonelessly with a nod at her dead companion.

Bolan slipped her Walther into his other pocket.

"He overplayed his part. Your people don't employ idiots. Whose house is this?"

"General Mahmoud's, as Yuri told you. All of what he told you was the truth. May I make myself a drink?"

"Go ahead."

She moved to the liquor cabinet. His eyes followed her, both as a precaution and as a man. She had a shape that moved nicely.

Bolan holstered the Beretta and returned to his bar stool.

Tanya poured a bourbon on the rocks and glanced over her shoulder at him.

"Care for one?"

"I'll stay thirsty. If you've got one general in your pocket, you've got more."

She turned to sip the drink and eye him over the rim of the glass.

"Why do you allow me to live?"

"You're worth more to me alive. Your partner would've been, also, but he was too stupid to realize it."

They studied each other speculatively, the tension almost palpable.

"You expect me to tell you everything I know," she said, "then you will turn me over to the *mujahedeen* and they will kill me slowly after they—"

"You can believe that or you can believe me," Bolan told her. "A group of generals plotting a coup with the KGB stage-managing as usual, huh?"

"You are neither romantic nor a fool," she responded. "You would not spare me because I am a woman. Your woman was not spared. What is it you want of me?"

"The informer inside the *mujahedeen*. You know who it is?"

"You threaten me with torture at the hands of these enemies of the people?"

"Your people maybe, not theirs. And I'll see that you're not tortured."

"As long as you live, perhaps, which will not be long in this land." She forced herself to look for an instant at what remained of Yuri Steranko, then she looked away and finished her bourbon with one swig. "All outsiders die in this hell, did you not know that? The cradle of civilization is to become civilization's deathbed. Ironic, is it not?"

She turned to slosh more bourbon into the glass, not as cleanly as before.

Bolan let her get drunk.

"You think like a poet."

She chuckled, only a little tipsy. She turned and some of the booze spilled from the glass. Bolan knew he was witnessing shock at what had happened to Steranko; the lady trying to camouflage normal human response with a mechanical manner as if everything was all right. Except the lady was no drinker.

"Every Russian is a poet. We are a soulful people. Why do you hate us so?"

"Don't be naive. Your country isn't exporting its poets or the soul of the Russian people."

She drained a third of the bourbon from the glass and turned away from Bolan and the corpse.

"I know nothing about an informer. That is the truth."

"Sure it is."

"I tell you, I know nothing!"

"Get specific, Tanya. Why did you toss that rope ladder when the soldiers were closing in? Why does the KGB suddenly want me alive? You started to tell me before. Those 'orders' you mentioned before Yuri decided to get stupid."

"We are prepared to make concessions," she told him. "I...was to make the initial contact. That is, Yuri and I. I was assigned only as his cover."

"Sure you were."

She turned to study the Man from Ice.

"I have never known a man like you before, Mack Bolan. I knew you would not be...average in any respect when I reviewed your dossier. You are very confident and sure of yourself. Perhaps too much so."

"Save the character study. You think you're smart giving me half-truths. You're not."

"It was hoped," she said, "that for...certain concessions, you might lend your capabilities to the generals'...cause."

"Try again. I'm already here as a favor to someone else. You know that from your informer."

She finished the last of the second drink and set the glass down with a clunk.

"The concessions to be offered...could, would extend to the faction you serve."

"I serve the good guys, Tanya, and your bunch don't come anywhere near that and never will."

"And that is your final answer to us?"

At that moment Grimaldi stepped back into the den from his recon outside the house, his Ingram in sight; a sidearm would have drawn no attention in the neighborhood beyond the walled property. Everyone in Iran had at least one gun. Grimaldi barely glanced at Steranko's sprawled corpse.

"How's it look, Jack?"

"I say we do it now. No signs of army or police activity in the vicinity. We're the other side of town from the pavilion. Guess they don't want to upset the muckety-mucks."

Tanya stepped forward.

"You have more to concern yourselves with than soldiers after assassins," she snapped. "My people will be out looking for me. General Mahmoud is a powerful man."

"So am I, sweetheart." Bolan capped the conversation. "Enough talk. Let's get out of here."

6

The withdrawal from Teheran had its moments. Three of them to be exact, when the Mercedes driven by Bolan was stopped at three different checkpoints, twice by Iranian Revolutionary Guard units, once by a roadblock of local police. Tanya was sitting next to Bolan and Grimaldi sat in the back seat, firearms hidden from view.

The hard guys who surrounded the Mercedes with aimed AK-47s and those who approached the driver of the Mercedes with drawn pistols at each stop could have been called thugs back in the States, Bolan reflected at the final checkpoint on the outskirts of Teheran. And here, where they enforced a dictator's martial law, they were hoods, too.

The falsified identification papers supplied by *mujahedeen* connections, and the Mercedes itself, bespoke authority that is more feared than respected in Iran as in all dictatorships. Bolan's olive complexion, high cheekbones and squarish jaw gave him a subtle Mediterranean appearance that could have easily been part or pure Iranian. It took Bolan and Grimaldi and their blond lady Soviet agent somewhat longer to clear the suburbs of Teheran, but not much. And that bothered Bolan.

"I would've thought they'd have the city sealed tighter than this," he mentioned to Grimaldi after the third checkpoint honcho waved them through.

"Now that you mention it," Grimaldi agreed.

The gut feeling that something wasn't right had not stopped gnawing at Bolan after they had left Mahmoud's house.

"As if nothing's happened," he considered aloud. "As if Khomeini hadn't been hit at all."

Tanya spoke up for the first time since the drive began.

"You pulled the trigger, did you not?" she queried Bolan. "You saw him die."

Bolan nodded, firing a cigarette with the dash lighter while he drove, trying to figure what his gut felt.

The lower-priced one-level adobe houses, the perimeter of Teheran, thinned away to become open country not long after the third checkpoint.

Bolan gave the well-tuned vehicle its lead on the sparsely traveled ribbon of blacktop as they continued southwest. He maintained close watch on the surroundings, using the inside and outside rearview mirrors.

A few more miles and it appeared they had pulled out of Teheran without complication.

Grimaldi stretched a jacket across the back-seat window to block the sun and curled up as best he could in what Bolan knew would be a catnap. He and Jack had been in enough combat zones together to know he could depend totally on the ace pilot for backup on a heartbeat's notice if they ran into trouble.

He wanted Jack rested when they reached the contact point with the *mujahedeen*. Bolan would catch a catnap of his own at that point. He needed Jack alert then to help keep Bolan's promise to Tanya Yesilov of protection from the *mujahedeen*, though Bolan felt he could trust the discipline with which Karim Aswadi commanded the insurgents' respect for their leader.

The Mercedes encountered little traffic along the highway, which cut along the base of the foothills. The few vehicles they passed were civilian, heading in the opposite direction, eager to make Teheran before sunset. The countryside was a lawless, treacherous no-man's-land after dark, not only because of the natural dangers of this wilderness. Outlaw bands, nomadic tribes, rebels, anyone hungry enough, willing to kill, roamed this inhospitable terrain; human animals of prey.

The woman beside Bolan sat staring straight ahead like a statue.

The highway skirted the salt flats outside Teheran, the ground deceptively solid, hard and smooth, though Bolan knew it to be a treacherous quagmire.

He traveled an indirect route to his contact point with the *mujahedeen*, more than an hour and a half additional driving time under the sun that was still blinding despite its gradual westward arc, but Bolan had no intention of leading anyone to Aswadi and his men.

No one followed them.

He concentrated on other things as he drove, allowing his postcombat tautness to relax while maintaining an eye-and-senses probing of their surroundings for danger beyond the Mercedes's windshield.

"Let's use our time, Tanya," he suggested. "Your orders to offer these concessions."

"You refused our offer," she replied quickly, turning to look at him. "I have nothing to tell you. I am your prisoner, that is all."

"Your superiors wouldn't think I'd consider throwing in with them," Bolan growled. "The concessions are for the *mujahedeen*. The KGB wants them in with your generals. So why are you uptight about where I'm taking you? You'll be able to make your pitch in person and from the premium on beautiful blondes in these parts, you might even charm Aswadi out of his common sense."

"Why is it you so disapprove of an alliance between your friends and ours?" she snapped.

"Compromise may achieve great goals. There is little time left for your *mujahedeen*." She glanced at him intently. "Khomeini is dead. That is all that matters now. General Mahmoud's force mobilizes as we speak."

"The general and his bunch are using you, lady," he told her evenly. "They think the Russians are a pack of godless dogs every bit as much as the *mujahedeen* hate you. The difference is that the generals are willing to sell out on their anticipated spoils for the help they need to pull off a takeover."

She turned to stare ahead again as Bolan gunned the German car, gas pedal to the floorboard, the speedometer steady near a hundred mph.

"I understand why you had to kill Yuri, though you must know you faced no real danger from him," Tanya said evenly.

"I guess he forgot people aren't supposed to point guns unless they intend to use them."

"The gun was meant to buy him time, not to kill you. Our orders regarding you were quite the opposite."

"Your cover assignment as his wife. Did you fall in love with him, Tanya? I need to know where I stand."

A heartbeat pause.

"I . . . became fond of Yuri. We . . . acted the role of husband and wife . . . completely only one time, but we were not compatible as lovers. Do you understand? We chose not to allow this . . . disparity to interfere with our work. I came to like and respect him, and now he is dead because of you."

"He brought himself to the moment of his death, Tanya."

Another heartbeat. Bolan's peripheral vision caught one pearl-sized tear squeeze from the corner of the lady's eye to ease down her left cheek. She did not blink it away.

"As do we all. You are right, of course. You, too, are a poet, Mack Bolan. This I did not expect from your dossier."

"Let's talk about you."

"I would prefer not to."

"You're young for this kind of work. Posing as an American housewife called for someone good, but you were meant as window dressing. A rookie assignment."

The intended jab got a response.

"You bastard. It will be my ass when I get home, as dear Ellie would say."

"Why did we get out of Teheran so easily, Tanya?"

She blinked in surprise at the question.

"You suspect me of being the bait to pull you into a trap? If you believe that, then by all means stop this machine immediately and I will gladly *un*bait the trap."

Bolan scanned the bleak landscape they were traveling through.

The countryside rated a look—the deserted ribbon of blacktop highway the only indication of today, all else unchanged since the dawn of time.

The highway curved along the northern tip of the endless sand nothingness of the Dashti-i-kavir, a trackless sea of thin sand blowing over rock and gravel, a desert rimmed by barren hills like the mesas of the American southwest, traveled only occasionally by caravans along a strip of sparse oases.

"I couldn't let myself turn you loose out here no matter what the circumstances," said Bolan. "I've seen you in action and they trained you well, first assignment or not. But there are too many cannibals prowling these hills. You'd run out of ammunition no matter how long you held them off, no matter how many you killed. Then they'd get you."

She nodded. Bolan saw a shiver course through her.

"I believe you. The *mujahedeen* we travel to meet, they will get you, us, out of the country?"

"That's the plan."

"And have you a plan for me after...if we leave this country alive?"

"I've thought about it. I plan to escort you safely beyond Iran's border and turn you loose, Tanya. And advise the proper agencies of your identity, so you'll have to stay out of the spy game whether you like it or not. Then you're on your own.

"You can return to Moscow and try to explain things and hope for the best from superiors who are not noted for accepting failure gracefully, as you must know, or you can choose from a million and one other points on this earth and go there."

"Defect, you mean," she snapped. "Your bourgeois capitalist mentality obviously cannot grasp real political and idealogical commitment." Then she seemed to hear herself and glanced at him contritely. "That is not true. You are a brave man, committed to your ideals, however wrong-headed."

"What you decide after we leave Iran is up to you," he finished, not taking his attention from his driving. "I just don't want your blood on my hands. Then we're even for you tossing that rope ladder."

"All very impersonal, is it not?"

"Stop it," he growled. "You said it already. We're enemies. Take the white flag and be grateful."

He had been closely watching the last several miles for the spot he remembered from the sketchy maps of the region he had seen the night before his and Grimaldi's penetration into Teheran.

They eased closer to undulating ridges to the west, the lowering sun already tinting their silhouettes a rosy hue.

Bolan slowed the sedan and steered from the highway onto a well-marked caravan track rising into shadowed patches of scrub brush at the desert's edge where hills began lifting higher.

Another forty minutes and they would reach the rendezvous point with Karim Aswadi and his unit of *mujahedeen*.

"Why did you ask me further about the proposed alliance between Aswadi's faction and General Mahmoud's?" asked Tanya. "Have you reconsidered our offer?"

"I also asked you about names I could use," Bolan countered. "What's wrong with a trade?"

She studied him then, briefly, intently, and seemed to decide.

"I think I know enough about you to offer you an additional inducement, Mr. Bolan. Yuri and I were attached to GRU—" Bolan knew this was the military intelligence arm of the KGB "—who will be providing the immediate support to General Mahmoud's forces. But when your presence was reported in the region, we were assigned a new control officer. KGB. Even Yuri was impressed. He is in Teheran now. His name is Major General Strakhov."

At the sound of Strakhov's name, Bolan ground his teeth in anger, working his jaw muscles. But he tried to keep his face impassive as he eyeballed a checkpoint in the descending gloom when the Mercedes topped the first rise.

They had set the roadblock well. Men stood with their backs to the setting sun at such an angle that the occupants of any approaching vehicle would only discern the forms of men in the shadows of a craggy ridge behind them.

Bolan slackened speed, not enough to draw suspicion from the checkpoint one hundred yards away. He downshifted as any more or less law-abiding citizen would be expected to.

Grimaldi sat up in back and immediately studied the approaching scene.

"Funny place for a roadblock. Wouldn't think an army unit would feel very safe out here from everything I've heard. They never move at night. Too many hostiles."

"You read my mind, buddy," Bolan growled.

He fed the car full upshifting throttle.

The men ahead had set up most of it, right. But only sufficient to fool most frightened civilians hurrying home to beat the dark, slowing them for a bothersome checkpoint without thinking until it was too late. But Bolan, himself an experienced role-camouflage expert, caught the little things like no radio antenna on the jeeplike vehicles. He knew that no patrol would be this far from civilization without damn good communications equipment to call for help, if needed.

Tanya got it then, too.

"Bandits," she whispered.

The five men in the road by the nose-to-nose vehicles reacted to the speeding-up approach of the Mercedes by scrambling for cover behind the vehicles, tracking automatic rifles at the oncoming car.

"Tanya, get down," Bolan instructed the lady. He steered with his left hand, unlimbering the AutoMag with his right in the final millisecond before hellfire erupted. "Here we go, Jack," he warned the man bracing himself with the MAC-10 at the open window in the back. "Pour it on hot and heavy. *Now!*"

7

Weapons blazed from both sides, dirty orange pencils of gunfire slivering to and from the rocketing Mercedes.

Automatic fire commenced from behind the bandit "checkpoint."

The ear-rattling thunder of the .44 hand cannon and angry popping from Grimaldi's Ingram reverberated through the interior of the Mercedes.

Bolan used the heel of his palm to wrench the steering wheel in sharp circles, almost flipping the car into a turn off the caravan trail without slackening speed.

Tanya obeyed Bolan's instructions and made herself as small as she could, hugging the floorboard of the car.

Projectiles smacked the Mercedes, angry hornets buzzing the rushing machine.

Then the enemy fire ceased as a tidal wave of loose gravel kicked up by the evasive maneuver descended like a small dust storm to blot out rifle-firing men behind the jeeplike trucks.

Bolan saw his .44 slug evaporate the head of one

back-falling highwayman, the red spray matching the sunset, while another guy curled over with a second navel, courtesy of Grimaldi.

Bolan powered the Mercedes past the roadblock vehicles, spewing up a cloud of dust that blanketed three surviving gunmen.

The three bandits opened fire at the car they heard barreling past before they could see what they were shooting at.

Bolan heard lucky rounds spang the coachwork.

A slug whined past the tip of Bolan's right ear, close enough to make it smart like a mosquito bite before drilling a spiderweb hole into the front windshield.

The dust dissipated and the red dots of stuttering assault rifles winked in the gathering dusk from behind.

The bandits squinted through the clearing dust swirls, tracking their blazing weapons on the receding car.

One of the gunners had his arms flung out like a bird trying to fly backward before toppling against a vehicle, then forward to the ground an instant after Grimaldi tossed a parting burst from his Ingram MAC-10.

The surviving two bandits held their fire long enough to feed fresh clips into their rifles, then realized the fast-departing Mercedes would be out of their range in another few seconds. They climbed into one of their vehicles, and the jeep-thing tore off in pursuit as if propelled from a catapult.

Bolan wheeled the Mercedes back onto the somewhat smoother strip of caravan trail.

Tanya remained crouched beneath window level, glaring at Bolan in anger and frustration.

"Please, give me my gun," she implored above the noise of the high-powering engine and wind whistling through the car. "I want to help!"

"Stay down."

Grimaldi positioned himself to return fire at the pursuing vehicle, which was already beginning to drop back, unable to match the Mercedes's effortless climb of another steep ridge.

"Save your energy, blondie," Grimaldi said, grinning. "We can outrun them yahoos with no trouble. The fun's over."

"Not quite," Bolan growled.

The two passengers twisted to follow his line of vision.

Grimaldi swore out loud.

Two desert vehicles that matched the pursuing one rocketed into view over ridges from either side of the road ahead. They were traveling at such high speeds they left the ground, airborne for several dozen feet until they each hit earth on a course that would intersect twenty yards ahead, the Mercedes boxed in between them and the vehicle coming in from behind.

The approaching machines appeared top-heavy

with men armed with rifles, the carriers jouncing full tilt across the rocky terrain to intercept the Mercedes within a minute or less.

"Five in each vehicle," Bolan growled, combat instincts sizing the options, simultaneously formulating a strategy.

"And two behind us. Those rifles they're carrying will eat us up," Grimaldi grunted, wiping sweat from his forehead. "This one could be kind of close."

"We need some of that firepower."

Bolan downshifted decisively, sharply brake-pumping into another high-speed turn, the powerful German car responding smoothly.

Tanya peered out the windshield at the springing of a well-orchestrated trap set for game that eluded the roadblock.

She braced herself and shouted above the rumble of the shuddering 180-degree spin.

"But how will we get their weapons?"

Grimaldi rode the centrifugal force of the turn, reading Bolan's mind, chuckling a response.

"Same way these creeps got 'em, doll. We take 'em."

Bolan upshifted, hammering down before the Mercedes completed its turn, the car speeding away from the two vehicles now closing in from behind.

The roadblock jeep had momentarily dipped from sight behind a ridge of the foothills and missed the action.

When the Mercedes reached a point fifty feet short of where the checkpoint vehicle would appear within a matter of seconds, Bolan steered and braked the Mercedes into a sideways stop.

"End of the line," he growled, already on the move, popping open his door.

He alighted from the Mercedes, the mighty AutoMag in his fist again, an extension of the warrior himself.

Grimaldi and Tanya darted away from the vehicle to beeline alongside Bolan from the Mercedes that now blocked the trail.

The desert vehicles converging side by side from two hundred yards away, twin juggernauts chomping up the distance, had their racing engines joined by the same sound telegraphing the approach of the third vehicle.

Bolan spun around to hold his ground in a springy, kneeling shooting crouch, the hand cannon aimed with both fists at the spot where the third vehicle careered into view over the ridge one hundred feet from Bolan.

Grimaldi and the woman swung around together, the blonde looking like she wanted her Walther PPK from Bolan more than ever.

The bandit driver reacted reflexively, jerking his steering wheel to avoid direct collision with the Mercedes. But he was not quick enough, and the vehicle clipped the front end of the German car, spinning it away under the impact of metal into slamming metal. The jeep's left front tire caught a rut, and the vehicle two-wheeled along for thirty feet or so, the driver fighting for control, his passenger screaming something frantic, the sound cut off when the jeep flipped, landing upside down and skidding until a wall of boulders stopped the grinding slide with another smash.

Bolan and his two companions charged toward the remains of the wreckage, its axles wrenched loose, dust settling over an unrecognizable, twisted pile of junk.

Tanya slowed back a few paces behind the Americans, sensing from their caution that one or both bandits could have survived the crash.

The vehicles barreling in from the west broke away from each other one hundred yards down the track, the drivers reacting to what had happened, advancing from two flanks instead of straight on.

Bolan sensed danger to his left through the haze of settling dust from the crash. He tracked the .44 to a whisper of movement before visual target acquisition and hammered a round from Big Thunder. The ugly *slap* sound of the head buster exploding living flesh and the thud told him at least one of the two in the checkpoint vehicle was out of play.

He approached the wreck, steam whistling from an overheated radiator the only sound.

He saw the bandit who had hidden behind the overturned hulk was about to fire. An AK-47 lay in his outstretched, quivering fingers.

The driver's broken remains were trapped where the steering column had pressed his head to jelly against hard ground during the vehicle's tumbling slide.

Bolan picked up the discarded AK. He stripped the bandit's military web belt of extra ammo clips.

"Oh-oh," he heard Grimaldi exclaim from the other side of the wreckage.

The flanking bandit vehicles barreled in for a blitz run from either side. The gunmen were ready to open fire as they closed the range in two or three more seconds, creating a cross fire from high ground.

Bolan hustled to where Tanya stood next to Grimaldi, who was straightening up after he grabbed a Russian-made portable grenade launcher. The weapon, wrenched loose from the bandit during the crash, was primed and ready to fire.

Bolan motioned to the rushing bandit vehicle on the left.

"Take 'em, Jack."

"With pleasure."

Bolan turned, tracking low on the vehicle the instant it flew into view from beyond the wreckage.

Tanya grabbed his arm.

"Please, my gun!"

He shook her loose and stroked a yammering burst from the AK-47 at the exact moment the jeep-load of bandits commenced firing. From Grimaldi's position the grenade launcher hammered a blast at the enemy.

Tanya hit the ground and hugged it as dozens of bullets from the jouncing jeep's open salvo sliced overhead.

The oncoming vehicle on Grimaldi's flank began to zigzag wildly the instant the driver and his gunners saw the cannon in Grimaldi's hands. Dismayed faces were swallowed in a thunderclap of a blossoming fireball that fragmented the vehicle and everyone in it, strewing the vicinity with flying debris, body parts and razoring shrapnel.

The other jeep on Bolan's flank flipped into a crazy forward end-over-end roll after the burst from Bolan's AK blew out its front tires. The bandits were thrown like discarded rag dolls, except for the driver who held on to the steering wheel until the vehicle finished its last roll, the steering column skewering him like a baited worm.

Two bandits did not stir from where they landed, their bodies twisted in grotesque angles. Bolan sprayed them anyway, the same fusillade raking two more highwaymen who dazedly gained their feet to look for their rifles. The autofire from the Executioner ended it and everything else for them.

Nothing moved in the wilderness around Bolan, Tanya and Grimaldi as echoes of the altercation receded into the distance. Then silence reclaimed the killground.

Tanya surveyed the aftermath with stunned disbelief. She brushed an errant strand of blond from her forehead, uncovering a not unattractive smudge along one high cheekbone.

"You gentlemen...are most incredible," she began in an attempt to not sound shaken. Then she gave up and said something to herself in Russian that Bolan did not hear.

He slammed a fresh clip into the AK, and swung the weapon's strap over his shoulder. Eyeing the surroundings, he fed a fresh magazine into the butt of the AutoMag, which he did not holster.

Grimaldi ambled over from where he had commandeered an assault rifle and extra ammunition from one of the dead around the stricken jeep.

He motioned with the rifle, indicating what remained of the bandits.

"Close, like I said."

"Too close, for them," Bolan said, nodding.

"And perhaps for us, as well," Tanya Yesilov added bleakly, as if hypnotized by the wasteland of desert and mountains surrounding them. Shadows of dusk spread across the ground like a dark stain toward bodies and the hulks of battered vehicles. "What will we do now?" she asked no one in particular.

8

Bolan and Grimaldi made an inspection of the fender-bent Mercedes, Bolan's AutoMag and Jack's rifle all the while fanning the descending gloom for any sign of danger.

Tanya accompanied them without a word, averting her eyes from the torn, bleeding human carcasses littering the area.

The German-made sedan rested at an angle across the caravan trail and bore little resemblance to the sleek machine of a short while ago, before it was plowed into by a bandit vehicle.

Bolan provided cover for Grimaldi, who crawled beneath the car for a closer look at the damage. Then he climbed behind the steering wheel, fired up the engine and drove the vehicle through a few turns and stops.

"Looks worse than it is," he called to Bolan. "It'll be a tough ride. The front end looks screwed up and we're minus a headlight. Back home we'd call a tow truck. Out here, I'd say we could make it maybe fifty miles, maybe half a mile."

"Let's go," growled Bolan. "Slide over, Jack.

I'll take the wheel. Tanya, you ride in front between us the rest of the way."

The woman did as she was told, saying nothing, avoiding eye contact with either man.

Bolan settled behind the wheel, and they continued on.

The Mercedes exhibited a severe alignment problem, and Bolan fought a pull in the steering wheel every inch of the way.

The bashed-in front end kept wanting to tug the vehicle off the caravan track, and the twisted fan kept hitting the radiator, sending up a loud racket in the silence of the rocky terrain. Occasional bursts of steam fogged the cracked windshield, and the Mercedes listed along at a maximum traveling speed of around forty mph.

Bolan curbed his irritation at not being able to move ahead faster.

So much to do. So little time. So many unanswered questions. A more or less straightforward mission complicated by far too many variables.

Variable number one continued to be the something dancing just beyond his conscious reasoning faculties, telling Bolan over and over that, sure, he saw Khomeini die through the sniperscope of the Weatherby on a Teheran rooftop that afternoon. Why then, Bolan wondered, did his subconscious keep pestering? Why did he continue to feel the vague, restless unease of a job left undone?

Other variables had a lot to do with it.

Like the Russian presence in Iran, which made about as much sense as Bolan's presence here, right; the single common cause shared by West and East. Everyone wanted this powder keg defused.

Variables.

A straightforward mission? Not anymore.

Nothing remained straightforward in Bolan's world anymore, if it ever had.

Certainly not in hellground Iran.

Variables.

Tanya Yesilov.

Blond, tough, nervy, unsure, afraid, dangerous. Especially dangerous, which is why Bolan had no intention of returning the lady's Walther PPK.

He had not stayed alive these many years of hell-grounding by handing out guns to women he did not trust, who had reason to hate his guts and everything he stood for, even if they had saved his life.

There was something about the tough yet vulnerable Tanya that Bolan liked, but he had liked her more as Ellie Talbot.

He wondered if he could believe any of what she had told him.

And *Strakhov*, the name she'd mentioned before Bolan had spotted the bandit roadblock.

Major General Greb Strakhov.

The KGB's most powerful official and the main focus of Bolan's KGB wars.

Strakhov had been the one to implement the

KGB operation that resulted in the attack on Stony Man Farm and the death of April.

Bolan owed Strakhov. In spades.

And Strakhov owed Bolan much the same, for on a previous mission into Russia, the Executioner had terminated a KGB savage, one Kyril Strakhov, only child of widower Greb Strakhov.

On news of his son's death, the KGB chief had relinquished loss of his last emotional connection to normal human feeling. He devoted every waking hour and the considerable power and resources at his command to an all-consuming hatred of Bolan that could only be satiated by the death of the Bastard in Black, as the world media had dubbed the Executioner.

Bolan, Strakhov.

Executioner and KGB Boss of Bosses, Cannibal of Cannibals.

Strakhov's cannibal colleagues cautiously whispered of their superior's having gone a bit mad over the Bolan matter, though this had no effect on the power Strakhov continued to wield.

Bolan and Strakhov.

Mortal enemies.

Each had on previous occasions, wrongly thought the other to be defeated, indeed dead, only to witness the other's reemergence at a most unexpected moment to renew their personal war.

Like now, in Iran.

The sun set, the air turned cool. Darkness cloaked the world.

The Mercedes wobbled along.

Bolan tried the still-functioning headlight, which was knocked out of focus by the collision, its beam now pointed directly at a spot four feet in front of the car to the right and nowhere else. But it and the silver, surreal glow of a quarter moon in a cloudless sky illuminated the trail that wound higher into rugged, barren terrain.

No one in the car had spoken during the past fifteen minutes.

A lot had happened.

And it wasn't over yet.

Bolan steered around a steep, curved grade, negotiating the turn so Tanya, between Bolan and Grimaldi, had to tilt against him, her hair in attractive, shoulder-length disarray. He inhaled the subtle womanly scent of her, sensed her exhaustion and excitement, before her reflexes straightened her away from the brief intimacy of contact. He had her attention.

"You were about to tell me something a while ago before we were so rudely interrupted," he reminded her.

"Was I?"

"Tell me about Strakhov."

She smiled a pure Mona Lisa, more to herself than to him, and in that instant Bolan wondered if she was in truth the complex proposition she appeared to be, or more so.

"I will tell you what I choose to tell you, when I choose to, Mack Bolan. I have my orders. I have offered you an inducement. How would Ellie Talbot say it? Oh, yes, the ball is now in your court.''

Grimaldi tossed Bolan a grin and a wink that said *she's all yours, buddy and good luck!*

"Some lady," he said, chuckling and making an unabashed appraisal of the lovely between them. Grimaldi was far too Italian to allow political ideology to stand in the way of his respectful appreciation of a beautiful woman.

Bolan gazed to their right, spotted what he was looking for and steered the Mercedes off the trail onto rougher ground.

"You're the one with the ball," Bolan corrected Tanya. "Let's see if you've got the balls."

He steered them over a rise in the rocky ground and for a few moments it looked as if the damaged Mercedes might give out on them. Then they topped the incline onto a sandy plain between two thrusts of higher land.

The old Achaemenid ruins shimmered in the dreamlike desolation on higher ground like a ghostly murmur from eternity. The ancient carved walls of brick and tile were eroded by millennia of wind and sand, the carving discernible, from another time, another world.

The Mercedes, as any vehicle approaching the ruins, had to pass through a natural culvert grooved through the rock by aeons of flash floods, the drain forming the only drivable approach to the ruins.

Bolan knew a dozen or more rifles were trained on the car he drove at a crawl, though his trained eye detected nothing. But yeah, he knew they were out there. He and Grimaldi had spent twelve hours with this unit, the People's Mujahedeen, temporarily base-camped at these remote ruins.

The Mercedes rattled to a wheezing stop.

Bolan turned off the ignition and headlight.

Shadowy shapes—six rifle-toting men—materialized from the gloom to stand directly in front of the car.

The camp in and around the ancient ruins looked unchanged from the night before when a team of Aswadi's men had met Bolan and Grimaldi and brought them there from across the Iraq-Iran frontier.

Security stretched several miles from the base, Bolan recalled from last night; teams of stationary and moving sentry teams in constant radio contact, some equipped with CIA-supplied infrared Night Vision Devices.

The night scene buzzed with muted voices around campfires near a dozen or more U.S. Army-surplus pup tents.

A man armed with an Uzi submachine gun stepped forward from the formation of five others behind him, aiming their rifles at the windshield of the Mercedes.

"Same routine as when we pulled in last night," Grimaldi noted. He glanced in all seriousness at the blonde beside him. "Here's where it gets close all over again, honey."

Tanya said softly, "You gentlemen saved my life when those bandits attacked us. We are even now, are we not; the debt repaid."

Bolan looked past the sentries to a figure approaching from the deeper gloom. Bolan knew the man had watched their approach, patiently biding his time before emerging to make a dangerous presence known.

"Good, you sound tough. You'll need that, Tanya. Here comes our host."

9

Bolan opened his door with deliberate slowness, careful not to alarm the *mujahedeen* fighters aiming their weapons at the car. But they reflexed into near flash point anyway, until the sentry with the Uzi stepped forward to wave a hand. The men behind him accepted that and retreated.

Karim Aswadi approached the Executioner and his companions.

The lean-muscled, middle-aged guerrilla leader, turbaned and in desert combat fatigues like his men, wore a pistol holstered butt-forward at his left hip. His features were reminiscent more of a scholar than a soldier.

Aswadi had been neither before the so-called "People's Revolution." He had become both in the terrible years since.

The riflemen surrounding the vehicle stepped aside respectfully for their leader.

Aswadi had conceived the intricate operation that brought the Executioner there to help them. Good, brave men in Karim's group would be all too willing to sacrifice their own lives to slay the religious dictator who enslaved the country. But no one in his group possessed the pure skill to breach the security behind which the Ayatollah hid.

The *mujahedeen* chief needed a specialist to plan and carry out an assassination that would destabilize the power structure long enough for those already in place to move and shift the balance.

Aswadi learned of Bolan's sympathy to their cause and the means by which to contact him after the Executioner's recent mission into Afghanistan. Bolan had aided the *mujahedeen* in that country in an audacious, stunning counteroffensive against the Soviets.

Bolan exchanged a firm handshake with Aswadi, then nodded introduction to the woman at his side.

"Karim Aswadi, Ellie Talbot, an American citizen. She helped us today in Teheran."

Aswadi bowed slightly from the waist, regarding her.

"Miss Talbot. This is...an unexpected circumstance. Americans are not as prevalent in Iran as before."

She cleared her throat, stalling to form a proper response.

Bolan spoke before she could.

"It's a long story, Karim. I hope you'll extend to Mrs. Talbot the hospitality you've extended to Jack and myself. I bear full responsibility for her during our stay with you."

The guerrilla leader nodded.

"It shall be. Accompany me, please. There are matters to discuss."

The *mujahedeen* warriors who surrounded and overheard this exchange parted again for their chief to pass, with Grimaldi and Tanya following closely.

The woman stared straight ahead as Aswadi led them up the incline toward the ruins. She felt glad to escape the staring eyes of the guerrillas, which she knew had to be evoked by more than the blondness of her hair in this corner of the world.

Do they suspect I am their enemy, she wondered, and knew some of them had to.

She suddenly felt none of the confidence she had tried to muster with Bolan and Grimaldi.

She wondered, as she hurried to keep apace with the long, purposeful strides of the men, if Bolan had seen through her, too. Or had she been a good-enough actress, make that good-enough agent, to work the number on him she had hoped to. She realized she had felt relieved when the American chose to lie to Aswadi about her. Having seen the fighters of the *mujahedeen* up close, she appreciated anew that her safety depended on this most unusual man, the stony one called the Executioner.

Nothing in training or her briefing on Bolan had quite prepared her for this strange man she felt beholden to, a feeling she tried to fight.

I must not forget my orders, she reproached herself. Yet I live because of him.

She felt a strange sort of liking for him, though she knew her orders were to kill Bolan. She wondered if this in fact could be the spark of the unsettling warmth she felt whenever the man spoke or in the few instances when they touched.

She assured herself it could not be lust, yet she knew deep down where the warmth felt good that lust was part of it. She had not had a man in months since the unsatisfactory experience with Yuri at the beginning of their assignment. And she'd had few men before that. But lust to her could only result from an appeal apart from sex.

The way this man spoke, though; his incredible life. She responded to all of these and when she realized this, she reprimanded herself angrily and told herself not to forget who she was. And what she must do.

Aswadi led them past charcoal fires where children crouched for warmth and women were roasting meager portions of lamb.

Suspicious, withdrawn eyes watched the three walk with their leader; hardship, determination and human misery pervading the atmosphere of the camp.

Sentries stood posted in two's at evenly spaced distances around the sparse remains of the ancient structure that Aswadi used as his personal quarters and office. Enough of the crumbling base at one section afforded a degree of privacy beyond earshot of the sentries who maintained an ongoing vigil of the night. They barely spared a glance for Aswadi, Bolan, Grimaldi and the woman as Aswadi motioned his guests to a small fire flickering near a corner of the wall beneath the star-splashed Iranian sky.

Aswadi gestured them to sit.

"Kindly accept what hospitality is mine to offer."

The *mujahedeen* leader poured tea into tiny enameled cups, passed the cups around, then lowered himself to sit cross-legged with them, eyeing Bolan.

"The first thing you should be apprised of, Karim," Bolan began, "is that you have a traitor in your group. Someone among you is informing to the Soviets or their proxies, or both."

Aswadi paused, teacup halfway to his lips.

"That cannot be."

"It is the truth, I assure you."

Karim set his cup down without tasting the tea.

"Who?"

"I'm sorry, I don't know. I only know you have been betrayed."

Aswadi stood abruptly.

"Then the traitor will be found at once."

He clapped his hands sharply.

One of the sentries stepped in.

Aswadi issued a series of sharp commands.

The guerrilla fighter nodded, saluted, turned and hurried away.

Aswadi returned to the others. He kicked dirt over the coals, dousing the fire.

Bolan and Grimaldi watched, unable to understand the language, Farsi, in which Karim and his man had communicated.

They remained alert, in tune with the night beyond the walls of the ruins, fingertips near their pistols, rifles within an arm's reach.

Bolan sensed no shift in the darkness, thanks to the *mujahedeen*'s security, but this Executioner knew better than most how the best of defense perimeters can be penetrated; he had done it himself many times. It had happened the night of the Stony Man Farm assault, the beginning of the end of Bolan's government connections, and he wondered how much he could trust Karim Aswadi.

"I don't know how the informer passes his information, Karim, but he may have already told them you're here."

Aswadi stared into the flickering, faint embers from the fire, deep in thought.

"We will move from here within the next two hours. I have ordered the fires put out, our women and children relocated at once well away from here where they will not be found until we withdraw and they join us."

"Question," said Grimaldi. "Your men could pull camp and be gone sooner than two hours. I'd guess your emergency pullout time at thirty minutes or less. Why two hours?''

Bolan fielded that one.

"Karim wants the traitor identified before moving to another camp.''

"I have charged my second-in-command to initiate this as we speak,'' the guerrilla chief acknowledged. "A handful of men, such as al-Hakim whom you met below, I trust implicitly. These men have served me long and well and have had countless opportunities to betray me in the past at times when it would have served our enemies well.

"You see, gentlemen, my organization differs from those radicals in Iran sharing the cause of Islam, extremist splinter groups as twisted by hatred as those who oppress us. They would slaughter the innocent, plant bombs in railroad stations and other public facilities to intimidate and destabilize the regime. I have never ordered an action against any other than military targets. I hope to defang the serpent rather than further victimize those for whom we fight. For this reason, I am high on the death lists of both the Russian and Khomeini's hoodlums.

"No, if someone in my command is a traitor, the godless ones would have used him to achieve my end long ago. We exist on discipline and trust. Each of my men has others he trusts, many related by blood and marriage or knowing one another since childhood.

"Al-Hakim is organizing a systematic investigation. Perhaps Allah will bless us with luck; the informer will be identified. If not...we move camp and pursue the traitor vigorously wherever we move."

Tanya Yesilov listened, fascinated, to the soliloquy.

"And when you know who the traitor is?"

"What would you think, dear lady?" Aswadi inquired in return, not unkindly. "He will tell us all that we demand of him, and he will be summarily executed." The *mujahedeen* leader addressed Bolan. "Tell me how you come to know with such certainty of a traitor among us?"

Bolan felt the blonde's eyes implore him and he hoped like hell he had it figured right.

"I lied to you a while ago, Karim."

"No, *please*!" the woman gasped, then glared at Bolan, eyes imploring more than ever.

Grimaldi looked ready to move at any cue from Bolan.

"I thought we were friends," Aswadi said, frowning at Bolan. "Brothers against a common enemy. How have you lied to compromise this between us, and why?"

"There is sufficient reason, Karim, and for my part we remain brothers-in-arms. This woman's name is Tanya Yesilov. She is a Russian KGB agent. She is my prisoner. I intend to escort her out of Iran when Jack and I have finished our work. I didn't want al-Hakim or your other men to know these things. I have guaranteed this woman her safety and ask you respect that.''

The tableau froze under the uncertain illumination of a quarter moon and stars in the crisp, endless dark.

Aswadi scrutinized the blonde.

''You have this man to thank for the breath you draw, young woman. Discipline and decency in the best of men would be tested when presented with the very personification of the reasons these decent people must survive like animals in the wilderness.''

Bolan looked at her.

''Make your pitch,'' he growled. ''This could be your only chance.''

Tanya turned to watch the night, her back to the men.

''You taunt me. Perhaps I deserve it.''

''I'd do it, lady,'' Grimaldi encouraged Tanya from where he carefully observed the unfolding scene.

Grimaldi remained near his rifle.

Tanya turned and said in a low voice, ''As you must know, Mr. Aswadi, the interests I represent—'' she faltered briefly ''—are attached, in an advisory capacity, to certain elements in Khomeini's military.''

Aswadi interrupted her with an irritable, derogatory gesture.

"Yes, yes, Mahmoud and his gangsters. We have our informants too, you see, miss."

"And did you know," Bolan added, "that Mahmoud wants an alliance with the *mujahedeen*? Their spy got word out about my involvement. Tanya and an agent posing as her husband had orders to approach you via me. The other agent is dead."

Tanya continued, "With the Ayatollah assassinated, the general's force is already mobilizing. We offer you concessions—"

Aswadi spit vehemently at the ground.

"Bah! You spin fables like Scheherazade. My force has attacked too many installations commanded by General Mahmoud in his capacity of loyal murderer for Khomeini. We have cost him dearly in equipment, men, prestige. The general and I are opponents to the death."

"I assure you—"

"Dear miss, you cannot assure your own survival through this night, so kindly spare me further elaboration on such ludicrousness. Mahmoud well knows and fears the power of my *mujahedeen* and of the threat we would pose were he to obtain power. They would hunt us down exactly as they do now under the guise of loyalty to their Ayatollah while their real objective is to destroy us for their own motives, before they take power. And in any event, these absurd overtures from Mahmoud may prove premature. Tell me, please, the details of the assassination."

Bolan did so concisely, sensing that his premonition about something amiss was about to be proven correct.

When Bolan finished, Aswadi said, "It is very strange. We monitor all radio transmission, public, official.... There is no mention whatever of the Ayatollah having been assassinated."

10

"Damn," Bolan growled under his breath.

Grimaldi emitted a soft whistle.

"Someone's up to slick tricks."

"There are only two ways it can be. Khomeini using a double for public appearances is one. I killed the double," Bolan said grimly.

Grimaldi agreed.

"It's been proved that Hitler and Churchill did it; plastic-surgery stand-ins. Castro supposedly still does it today for big open-air addresses and the like," the pilot added.

"They clamped a blackout so fast at the pavilion today, even the witnesses won't be sure of what they saw by tomorrow," Bolan pointed out.

"You mention a second possibility," said Karim.

"Strakhov," Grimaldi suggested.

"Strakhov," Bolan acknowledged. "Whether I got the real Khomeini today or not, the KGB or someone for them could be blacking the news out as a power play."

Aswadi considered, then shook his head.

"We would have heard something. They could not conceal the assassination completely. We have people highly placed in the Majlis and every official agency."

"Then they are using a double of the Ayatollah," Bolan growled. "It's a reasonable precaution considering all the people who want him dead. If there is an assassination, the body is whisked away and if the public is told anything, it's that an unsuccessful attempt was made."

Grimaldi grunted.

"If our objective is to take out Khomeini, I'd say this throws a real wild card in the deck."

Aswadi turned to Tanya.

"Perhaps our Russian friend knows something of this. I warn you, miss, I am not a cruel man, yet if these entrusted to me and those I fight for are in danger, I shall resort to whatever measures necessary to make you tell us—"

"I know nothing of any of this!" the blonde insisted. "I am little more than an amateur, sent as role camouflage for the operative, Yuri Steranko, and Steranko had no knowledge of any of this, I assure you."

"The amateur bit is exaggerated but not much," Bolan said to Aswadi. "Steranko was lower echelon, too. Strakhov? An organization man. I know that firsthand. He wouldn't allow his agents into the field, if he knew of our intentions to hit Khomeini, without a full briefing of anything he had on the possibility of a Khomeini stand-in. Strakhov would consider it foolish to send the woman and Steranko in blind like that, and Strakhov is not stupid."

"Even if I accept your reasoning," Aswadi replied, not turning from the woman, his expression hard, stoic, "there is the matter of the KGB informant."

Bolan casually positioned himself between Tanya and Aswadi. He tossed Grimaldi an almost imperceptible nod.

Jack eased back slightly, absently hefting and canting the AK-47 across his left arm.

"I promised Tanya she would be safe with me," Bolan reminded Aswadi.

"She is our enemy," the *mujahedeen* chief insisted. "She knows much that would benefit us greatly in our struggle."

"We must compromise and understand each other," Bolan countered. "And you need me, Karim, more than ever if our idea is right about what happened in Teheran today. The real Khomeini may be alive and laughing into his beard right now at what fools he made of us."

This got Aswadi's attention as Bolan intended it to.

The *mujahedeen* commander relaxed, easing the tension.

Bolan stayed between Aswadi and Tanya, hoping Aswadi would not pursue this stubbornly. He did not want to oppose Karim but would take his chances with Jack and Tanya in the hills before betraying his promise of safety to the woman.

"What shall we do?" Aswadi asked.

"The woman?"

"I must trust your judgment, against my wishes. Her true identity shall remain a secret from my men, as you wish. But hear me, Bolan. You shall pay with your life if this enemy brings about the death of even one of my people, directly or through design. She shall pay. You shall pay. With your lives. On my word of honor."

"I accept those terms, Karim."

"Then our conversation is ended for now. I must supervise the investigation for an informant. You three will have some time to rest if you wish."

"I wish," Grimaldi said, nodding. "It's been one hell of a day."

"There is a tent a short distance beyond this wall for messengers from other units who spend the night. It is unoccupied," said Aswadi. "You have ninety minutes before we move camp. I will see you are not disturbed."

"When you've set up a new base camp," said Bolan, "we must formulate an effort to nullify whatever Khomeini's people managed to accomplish today."

"Something inside warns me that I am making a terrible mistake by trusting this woman," Aswadi stated stonily. "And yet I acquiesce, and thank you for agreeing to see this through with us."

"I don't like puzzles," Bolan growled. "I want to make quick work of this one."

"And so you have my gratitude." Aswadi turned to leave, casting one parting glare at the blonde who remained standing behind Bolan. "Would that you had not seen fit to so endanger your mission and our lives as you have."

Aswadi left them.

"Let's find that tent," said Bolan.

The tent, U.S. Army surplus to match the others, was pitched well away from where the encampment buzzed with low-keyed, earnest activity, the dependents already vanished into the night during the conversation with Karim.

Bolan watched the proud, forceful figure of Aswadi stride toward the area where al-Hakim had assembled the guerrilla fighters. Then the Executioner turned back to Jack and Tanya.

The tent, pitched flush against a young oleander for shade during the day, looked big enough for one person.

Bolan knelt, lifted back an end flap for a cursory look inside, then held the flap aside for Tanya.

"Chivalry dictates," he said, indicating the inside of the tent to her.

She remained standing.

"I am not tired. I shall remain outside."

"Don't make a scene," Bolan advised quietly. "I'm tired and when I close my eyes, I want to know where you are and where you'll stay."

She did not budge, glaring defiantly.

"And what makes you think I shall stay anywhere?"

"You're forgetting, Tanya," Grimaldi chided her in mock reproach, "you're a prisoner."

She started to bristle a response.

Bolan chose that moment from his kneeling position to grab Tanya's left ankle and tug the lady sharply off her feet.

She uttered a startled shriek, landing half in, half out of the tent. She started struggling wildly, but Bolan had already reached behind him and pulled his handcuffs from his belt.

He yanked her in after him and snapped one cuff around the slender trunk of the tree, the other to her wrist, effectively handcuffing Tanya in place.

He continued out the opposite end of the small tent and dropped both end flaps back into place, which did nothing to dim the red-hot blast of good old American swear words screamed at Bolan with inspired anger.

"Save your strength," he growled at her, stalking away. "You'll need it when we pull out."

Grimaldi sat nearby against a smooth boulder, grunting agreement as Bolan strode over to him from the noisy pup tent.

"I don't figure Aswadi is the type of guy to waste money on chartering us a couple of buses," Grimaldi said.

The snarling hellcat in the tent tapered off into silence.

Bolan eased himself down to sit on a rock across from Grimaldi. Bolan couldn't disguise the weariness of the involuntary sigh he emitted as he allowed himself to semirelax for the first time in seventeen tough hours.

"Grab some shut-eye," Grimaldi offered. "I'll take first watch."

"Thanks, Jack, but if our charge in that tent decides to pull anything, it will be in the next half hour. She'll be asleep after that, if she isn't sawing 'em off already."

"Well, if you insist," Grimaldi said. "Wake me in thirty."

He made himself comfortable and closed his eyes, already drifting off.

Bolan chuckled to himself, feeling better just from the chance to slow down, however briefly.

He fired up a cigarette and quietly edged over to the tent. Without a sound he crouched at the end flap from under which Tanya's wrist extended, securely handcuffed to the tree. He heard the deep, steady breathing of a person asleep or of someone pretending to be, and either way suited him.

He returned to the position that offered a view of the tent and where Jack slept sitting up.

Bolan allowed himself to relax without letting down his watch of the night around them.

He wondered what the hell to make of Tanya Yesilov.

Or Ellie Talbot.

Or whoever and whatever his lovely blond prisoner might really be.

THE THREE HELICOPTER GUNSHIPS lifted off in formation like bloated primeval insects. The throb of the revving rotor blades rumbled through the desert night, creating a turbulent backwash of swirling dust on the ground behind and below.

General Mahmoud watched the night swallow the war birds as they gained altitude. He barely noticed the billowing dust swirls those around him turned to avoid. He knew no world but that of the desert and his oneness with it and its laws.

Major Kravak turned again with the other three men of the group as the turbulence subsided. Kravak glanced at the luminous dials of his wristwatch. The Soviet army's GRU liaison "advising" Mahmoud's force wore piglike features and a coarse manner Mahmoud found nearly intolerable.

I will enjoy killing this one when the time is right, the general thought yet again.

"Precisely on schedule, General." Kravak spoke accented English. "I expected no less. You are certain of Aswadi's position?"

"Nothing is certain in Iran these days, my dear Major."

Mahmoud concealed his resentment, his hatred; the humiliation of deferring to this Russian pig he outranked. When the time is right, he reminded himself again. Very soon. . . .

"If those gunships locate and deal with Aswadi and his pack of jackals, all the better," Kravak snarled. "In any event, our gunships have more than enough time to rendezvous with your force for the assault on Lavizan."

"We begin for Teheran at once," said Mahmoud.

He snapped orders at the three officers, co-conspirators in the Russian-supported plot to overthrow Khomeini and install military rule headed by Mahmoud.

Tomorrow, or the day after, thought Mahmoud, and the time will be at hand; the godless Russian "advisors" would be dealt with, eliminated, and the power would belong to Mahmoud and only those to whom he delegated his power. The law of the desert, truly; Mahmoud knew it well: the right of power to those with the strength and cunning to claim it.

His officers departed toward the cluster of one dozen army troops secretly loyal to him, combat equipped, carefully chosen, experienced infantrymen armed with Kalashnikov rifles.

The general and Major Kravak watched the

troops board the eight-wheeled BTR-6 armored personnel carrier idling near the landing pad of the military compound commanded by Mahmoud.

Kravak mirrored a mutual loathing for the Iranian.

"You are certain your superiors suspect nothing?"

"I have few superiors," Mahmoud reminded him. "Redeployment of troops as I see fit is unquestioned, attributed to our Ayatollah's war with Iraq, ceasefires notwithstanding. We operate under a cloak of complete secrecy, Major, and by this time tomorrow it will not matter. When we are certain Khomeini is dead, we will move in the open as will those in Teheran who await my orders. Then it shall be done."

"An unfortunate mixed blessing, this intelligence report regarding Khomeini's use of impostors, coming to us from your informant in Aswadi's organization," Kravak groused. "If your informant is discovered and forced to divulge this information to the *mujahedeen*—"

"I have considered the possibility," Mahmoud interrupted. He experienced a growing excitement as the vehicle full of rebel troops grumbled to life. "I anticipate confronting Aswadi's force, Major, particularly if the man Bolan is with them."

Kravak stared off in the direction of the departed gunships.

"Bolan is out there," the GRU man snarled.

"Major General Strakhov himself will order my promotion at the very least when I report liquidation of the Executioner under my directions. Then there will be no more filthy assignments to hells on earth such as this one."

Mahmoud ignored the insult, as always.

"And the woman you spoke of? The KGB operative with Bolan in Aswadi's camp?"

Kravak shrugged.

"A sacrifice of war. I remind you, General, you have your objective and I most assuredly have mine. At the top of my priorities is the extermination of Mack Bolan. We have one hundred experienced desert soldiers in armored vehicles with air support." The Soviet nodded to himself. "He will not die easy, but he is an outsider outnumbered and outgunned in a hostile land. The Executioner will not escape death this night."

11

Bolan snapped awake moments before he heard al-Hakim's muted approach.

Grimaldi pulled his rifle around, tracking on Karim Aswadi's second-in-command.

Bolan stood, appearing fresh from the half sleep interrupted by al-Hakim, whose first impression of this unusual American reconfirmed itself when he saw Bolan automatically reflex into a combat crouch. The impressive handgun remained holstered at Bolan's hip, but the big foreign fighting man appeared ready to confront Allah or the devil himself, thought al-Hakim.

Bolan had been roused from his rest not by al-Hakim, but by the barely noticeable first reaction of Grimaldi when he saw al-Hakim striding toward them from the knot of Aswadi's *mujahedeen* in the nearby darkness.

"Karim requests your presence."

He had met these men briefly when the Executioner and Grimaldi arrived yesterday.

Grimaldi lowered his rifle.

"Find your spy, al-Hakim?"

"It is urgent that you accompany me without delay." Al-Hakim glanced to the tent. "The woman, too."

"I feel safer with this lady in sight, anyway," Bolan said.

Grimaldi and al-Hakim accompanied Bolan as they walked toward the tent.

Bolan produced a key for the cuffs.

The three men saw something wrong when they reached the tent: the handcuff snapped to the base of the oleander coiled empty upon itself like a metal snake, dully reflecting the moon glow.

Grimaldi swore.

"I think we goofed."

Bolan crouched, tossing back end flaps for a fast look into the tent, then rejoined Grimaldi and al-Hakim, who knew what happened by Bolan's grim expression.

"The damn fool!" Bolan growled heatedly, scanning the moon-tinted gloom around them. "I thought she had more sense. She stands one chance in a thousand of making it out there."

"She must've sprouted wings," Grimaldi grunted. "I never heard a thing, and I was damn well listening and watching."

"I know you were, Jack." Bolan retrieved the cuffs, studied them a second and looped them back beneath his jacket. "She's good, that's all, and small boned and well trained. Muscle control and patience and maybe some spit got her free, and when our heads were turned at just the wrong moment, she made her break."

"What do you think she'll do now? Where can she go?"

Bolan's fists clenched at his side. He scanned the night-shrouded, hostile, uninhabitable hill country.

"If I knew that, Jack, I'd be out there right now trying to intercept her and bring her back."

Al-Hakim stepped forward.

"I regret to stress the urgency of Karim's request."

"When it rains, it damn well pours," Grimaldi grumbled without rancor, "even in Iran."

Bolan pulled his attention from the futility of contemplating which direction the woman could have taken in her escape and indicated Grimaldi to accompany him.

"Lead the way, al-Hakim."

The freedom fighter led them past the ruins and the doused fires where a sprawling camp had buzzed with life less than two hours ago.

Al-Hakim reflected for a moment on this man, Bolan. The guerrilla knew from his tenure as university head librarian before the revolution, when Americans had often come to the library, that their stoic discipline in the face of adversity constituted a national trait in a people al-Hakim happened to respect very much—the principle reason Khomeini's goons had ousted al-Hakim from his job before he and his family were placed on the death list. He thought this man Bolan and his friend Grimaldi personified the best in what America had to offer.

He led the Americans to a secluded spot of murky shadow, separated from the concentration of *mujahedeen* behind a dip in the terrain near a cluster of gnarled trees.

Aswadi and two of his men appeared to be examining one of the trees. Aswadi turned to Bolan, al-Hakim and Grimaldi stepping aside.

"Where is the woman?" Karim demanded. Then he pointed to a figure in guerrilla garb sitting at the base of the tree. "He will only speak to her."

Bolan and Grimaldi saw a man, his back arched against the pressure of a curve-bladed dagger protruding from his neck, his blood-soaked clothes indicating he had been sitting painfully like this for some time.

The man's eyelids flickered like a fading pulse.

"Who did this?" Bolan asked.

He crouched beside the dying man.

Aswadi and the others crowded in close.

"His name is Mezhabi," said the guerrilla commander. "My men noticed his absence. They searched when no one could account for his whereabouts. They found him here, as you see him. He is a new recruit to our ranks. Inside his wallet, we found a paper on which were written some numbers. I recognized them as telephone numbers,. in Mezhabi's own handwriting. I have often used those numbers to contact sympathizers to our cause, those who feign loyalty to the oppressors. The numbers are in government offices in Teheran, and two I know to be organizations sponsored by the Soviets.'' Aswadi spat angrily upon the daggered man. ''This man is our traitor.''

''Or a diversion for the real one.'' Bolan looked into fogged eyes of a dying man. ''Mezhabi, do you recognize me?'' The eyelids flickered.

''B—Bolan....'' Crimson drool leaked onto a quivering, grizzled chin; the voice a faint wheeze. ''Tanya....'' Mezhabi labored hard for each tortured word. ''Must...speak....''

''Why?''

''She...can help....''

''Tanya can't help herself. She's gone. I don't know where she is. Who did this to you?''

Mezhabi's blood-specked mouth tremored.

''I...do not know the name...I...attempted to contact...the woman....''

''You helped her escape?''

''No...sentries...questioned me...suspicious...searched me...found wallet...did this... tried to kill me....''

''An example,'' Aswadi intoned gravely, ''to any who consider betrayal. It is good this one's death is particularly slow.''

Bolan grasped the dying man's shoulder in an effort to prevent him from slipping into unconsciousness.

"What did you have for Tanya? Tell me."

The dying man coughed, pink spittle bubbling across trembling lips.

"Khomeini . . . they know . . . ."

The murmured words faded like weak radio reception, becoming more and more disjointed, in a mind already gone behind glassy eyes that rolled back until only the whites showed.

"Tell me, Mezhabi," Bolan commanded brusquely.

The dying man's body spasmed.

Bolan leaned close to pain-racked features distorting into a hideous rictus. He heard a whisper soft as a baby's sigh riding Mezhabi's last expelled breath.

"*Lavizan* . . . tomorrow . . . ."

Mezhabi's rigid sitting position relaxed.

12

Grimaldi watched the dead man topple sideways.

"No tomorrow for that dude, whoever we have to thank."

Aswadi said, "Allah is to thank, the instruments of His will of no further consequence to us." He turned to Bolan. "What did Mezhabi whisper to you as he died? Where is the woman?"

"Mezhabi said 'Lavizan,'" said Bolan, "and the word 'tomorrow.' I assume since he spoke in English, Lavizan is the name of a person or place."

"Barracks in northeastern Teheran for the shah's troops," Aswadi answered thoughtfully. "Dissidents were interrogated, tortured there before the revolution. After Khomeini took power, the walls of Lavizan glistened with the lifeblood of government Javidan guards killed during the take-over."

"Why would Mezhabi refer to it?"

"I am uncertain." The guerrilla leader frowned. "At first the buildings were used to detain and eliminate people following the overthrow but it has been some years since the mass purges. Lavizan has fallen into disuse, most of Khomeini's forces and expenditure channeled into the Iraq problem. There may be a skeletal guard and nothing more.''

Bolan stood from beside the body, having formulated a few ideas of his own.

''I'd say there could be a whole lot at Lavizan, but not for long.''

''Clarify, please.''

''The other things Mezhabi said,'' Grimaldi put in, '' 'Khomeini' and 'they know.' Think he meant the real Ayatollah, or another double?''

''Let's piece it together,'' Bolan suggested. ''Mezhabi dies trying to get a message to the woman, the same message he gave us.''

''Unless the guy checked out a real pro,'' said Grimaldi, ''and everything he told you is mucho crapola.''

''The woman,'' Aswadi barked. ''You have not explained her absence.''

''She can be explained when we have the time,'' replied Bolan icily. ''If Mezhabi's 'tomorrow' means anything, we don't have a second to spare.''

''Do not dismiss the matter,'' Aswadi insisted. ''I have warned you—''

''Tanya is the only one who needs to worry about where she is right now, not us.'' Bolan severed Aswadi's sentence like a blade. ''There is no Soviet ground presence in the area or you'd know about it, and we'd already be gone. I know that much about you and your men. There being no enemy ground force in the area, the only ones she's likely to run into out there are bandits, unless tomorrow's heat and no water get her first."

Aswadi studied the American.

"Your concern for the woman is genuine."

"And there's not a damn thing I can do for her," growled Bolan. "Are we friends, Karim, or must I continue alone?"

"If she causes the death of one of my men—"

"We've been through that. We've got no options open to us except to fight this one on the heartbeat with what we've got. We lose time wasting words."

Aswadi nodded.

"We understand each other. I honestly hope, my friend, that you have not erred in your judgment, that I will not be compelled to kill you."

Grimaldi considered the corpse.

"If what Mezhabi had was important enough to risk his life to tell the woman, I'd put bucks on it having everything to do with what happened in Teheran this afternoon."

"Or more precisely," said Aswadi, "the possibility of there being more than one Khomeini; a dispiriting notion but probably true."

"If we accept what Mezhabi died saying," said Bolan, "and the idea of a systematic deception with one or more Khomeini doubles, a highly organized operation, the 'they' Mezhabi spoke of has to be the crew Khomeini has running the operation the way they did at the pavilion today. It has to be top secret. The whole idea is to keep the old bird safe from the public *and* those who wield power with him. He can't afford to trust anyone.''

"If Mezhabi knew about the doubles,'' said Grimaldi, ''that means the Russians know.''

"And if Khomeini's impostors do in fact operate from the Lavizan barracks,'' Aswadi asked Bolan, "can you surmise why Mahmoud has not attacked? If the Russians know, they would have certainly ordered Mahmoud to strike. They, too, wish the Ayatollah destroyed.''

"Your plans for the takeover of the government after the assassination,'' said Bolan. ''What's the status of your people?''

"Ready to implement at the moment of the Ayatollah's demise. We have units in the outlying regions and towns, fully prepared for the necessary show of force, but years of careful preparation should accomplish our ends in the confusion that will follow Khomeini's death.''

"Why not let Mahmoud attack the Lavizan barracks and maybe hit the real Ayatollah,'' Grimaldi suggested, ''then implement the *mujahedeen* takeover? Can the death of one man matter all that much if everything else is ready to roll?''

"If the man is Khomeini,'' the Iranian assured Grimaldi, ''it means everything. The madman has cast a spell over this country to the brink of ruin. When the spell-caster is destroyed, the spell will be broken.''

"The Russians are working their schedule, not ours," Bolan told them. "If we accept Mezhabi's 'they know' and piece it with the dying, 'tomorrow,' we could already be too late."

"The Khomeini punks handling the impostor deal know the Russians and Mahmoud are hip to the Lavizan setup," Grimaldi explained. "Mezhabi learned Khomeini's operation plans to git before anyone tries to hit."

"We have to assume Mahmoud and the Russians have more than one source of information," Bolan concluded, "and will have learned from another source what Mezhabi wanted to tell them. Karim, we should arrange protection for our women and children and be on the move back into Teheran at once. If Mahmoud knows Khomeini's crew is planning to relocate tomorrow, he'll strike tonight, and that means a military takeover."

Aswadi responded, not to Bolan but to al-Hakim and the others of his command, orders in Farsi that sent al-Hakim and the men snapping salutes and scurrying off toward the concentration of fighters.

Aswadi said in English to the two Americans, "We begin immediately for Teheran."

"Transportation?" Grimaldi asked.

"There is a refugee camp unknown to the army, several kilometers from here," Karim explained. "They have vehicles and offer us use of them when necessary. We will be in Teheran no later than midnight."

They headed toward the guerrilla unit already dispersing in the gloom.

"We can use your five best men," said Bolan. "Fewer men will be a damn sight easier to get into Teheran."

Grimaldi snorted.

"We stand a good chance if their checkpoints are as shabby as they were today. This time of night they'll be worse."

"There will be much killing if we encounter General Mahmoud," Aswadi said. "We chance the ending of our lives, you and I, Bolan, guided by the disjointed ramblings of a dying traitor and sheer conjecture. We must consider the possibility of the true Ayatollah Khomeini being nowhere near the old barracks in Teheran."

"And I hate to point this out," Grimaldi said, "but how would we know the real Ayatollah if we find one and what if we find more than one?"

"If we don't find His Royal Madness at Lavizan, we will learn his exact whereabouts. We'll hit *him* tonight, also. Then you can implement your take-over, Karim. If it's what we expect, the crew at Lavizan has to know where Khomeini is at every minute, even if no one else does, for the logistics to run as smoothly as they did today."

They reached a spot where Aswadi stopped to hoist his sleeping bag and field pack across his back.

Bolan noted nearly half the guerrilla force already gone, vanished into the night with all their gear, blending soundlessly with murky, rugged terrain in the short time since Karim had issued the command to pull out.

Bolan saw al-Hakim pause in organizing and preparation of the dependents for their march to the refugee camp for transportation. Aswadi's second-in-command was engrossed in an animated exchange with someone, the staticky reception of the two-way radio he held indiscernible to Bolan. Then al-Hakim ran toward them, shouting in Farsi. His voice was drowned out before he reached them, cut off by a roaring man-made thunder bursting from the Stygian gloom.

In the instinctive scramble of everyone on the ground to the nearest cover, Bolan tagged the ruction as incoming gunships. He saw the death birds heavy with 40mm cannons and machine guns the instant the in-zooming choppers opened up.

Explosions and shrieks of pain shattered the night as hellfire whistled in, blowing men apart, bursts of the firestorm tracking directly at Bolan, Aswadi and Grimaldi.

13

Bolan, Aswadi and Grimaldi fanned out in separate directions to escape the lethal hail of bullets from the Huey gunships. They swooped in low overhead, each chopper strafing the camp as *mujahedeen* fighters sought cover.

As he flung himself away from the path of a fire-spewing Huey, Bolan glimpsed one of the fast-sequenced detonations of impacting rockets evaporate the running figure of al-Hakim, Aswadi's right-hand man.

The closest gunship soared past Bolan directly overhead, its incoming fire plowing the earth where Bolan and Grimaldi and Aswadi had stood moments ago.

Bolan came out of his roll, rifle tracking around toward the death birds that were blitzing the night everywhere around him.

Grimaldi and Aswadi picked themselves up from the ground several hundred feet from Bolan, both men swinging their weapons around.

Another death-dealing rocket leaped from a speeding Iranian air force gunship as the Hueys completed their first pass before rotoring out of range of the riflemen on the ground.

Bolan saw the trajectory of the parting shot with no time to shout a warning, his insides shuddering when the 40mm-round burst between Bolan and where Grimaldi and Karim stood, too near to Jack.

Aswadi dived for cover.

Jack started to.

The blast flung Grimaldi into the air, arms and legs outflung, his rifle flying from his fingers.

No, Bolan's mind screamed silently.

He triggered a burst from the AK-47 appropriated during the clashes with bandits earlier that night, ceasing fire when he realized venting blind rage did not change the fact that the gunships had already buzzed well beyond rifle range.

He turned and hurried to the spot where an unmoving Grimaldi lay sprawled. Bolan and Karim reached him together. He saw Jack's left leg twisted unnaturally underneath the right leg and carefully turned him over.

The surviving guerrillas also held their fire on the choppers.

Shadowy figures filtered among the fallen, the survivors regrouping, hauling the wounded to cover.

The gunships, without flight lights, broke formation, their rumble of racing rotors and engines withdrawing.

The Hueys banked against the black sea of stars, circling, coming in again in a high-speed, three-across battle formation, seconds from another assault on the scattering ground force.

Grimaldi groaned, semiconscious.

The surge of relief Bolan felt at the sound of his buddy's voice died when he saw the blood-soaked mess of Jack's unbroken leg.

Bolan gingerly locked his arms beneath Jack's knees.

"Grab him," he shouted to Aswadi above the advancing thunder.

The guerrilla leader helped lift the wounded American, the two men hustling low, carrying Jack with them toward an inky clump of boulders five yards away.

The incoming choppers opened fire, cannons and mini-guns wide open.

Sequenced explosions delivered destruction around Bolan, Aswadi and the man they toted.

Twin streams of automatic fire erupted from the middle chopper, and geysering lines of 5.56mm slammers rippled in, too late for evasive or defensive maneuvers without Bolan and Karim having to drop the seriously injured man.

The *mujahedeen* on the ground vainly returned fire from their positions of concealment.

Bolan noted two grenade launchers among the guerrillas firing without luck.

One fighter saw the predicament of Aswadi and

the two Americans. The man raised one of the launchers, triggering a grenade at the gunship tracking in on the duo and their human cargo.

The splattering geysers of autofire eating up the distance stopped abruptly less than ten feet from the three men, who were caught in the open.

Bolan and Aswadi crouched behind the cover offered by a cluster of rocks, hurriedly but carefully lowering Grimaldi on his back.

The Hueys slammed by overhead, the choppers to either end of the formation raining steady blankets of bullets and explosions down upon the *mujahedeen*, but with less accuracy than before.

The center Huey maintained its buzzing course at nearly rooftop level for two or three seconds without resuming fire. At a distance of a quarter mile the chopper suddenly blossomed into a blinding fireball explosion that dwarfed the other sounds of war, the flame ball diving sharply. The secondary explosion of its crashing impact into the ground flared a moment later.

The fighter with the grenade launcher caught a pulping double hit from a gunner in one of the remaining two choppers.

The gunships banked off to circle for another of what Bolan knew would be continuous strafe runs until the dead bodies of all these men dotted this hillside.

Guerrillas shouted to one another in Farsi through the dark as the rotor and engine racket of the Hueys diminished again, the freedom fighters taking to higher ground, slowed by carrying their wounded, double-checking men felled, the scene illuminated by flickering flames of the downed chopper.

Bolan worked fast using a special length of rope, intended for silent killing, which he yanked from one of the pockets in his jacket.

He tied the short rope tightly around the upper thigh of Grimaldi's blood-soaked leg, which glinted black in the moonlight like spilled oil.

Aswadi snapped a branch from a nearby tree. The Iranian looped the rope, twisting the branch quickly into a tourniquet to stem the pulsing spurts of blood from shrapnel wounds.

The rotoring clamor of the approaching choppers came in with less bluster and speed this time, the crews reacting to the loss of one of their own with some caution but not much, tilting in low like scavengers buzzing the earth for food.

Grimaldi lightly touched Bolan's shoulder.

"Thanks, big guy. . . but I think maybe I bought it. . . this time. . . ."

"Shut up, Jack. Keep your head down."

Aswadi moved to withdraw from the rock shield that concealed them from the choppers already firing on straggling *mujahedeen* unable to reach cover, the night splitting apart with more slaughter.

"I will bring our medic."

Bolan stopped him with a restraining motion.

"Let the choppers pass. They're sighting with infrared. We don't need you and Jack both down."

Grimaldi cursed in rapid Italian.

The gunships flew in closer, turret-mounted miniguns yammering only sporadically now, but Bolan could see shredded corpses of guerrillas toppling as strobelike flashes of devastation cracked the night. A smattering of ineffectual rifle fire returned from the ground.

Aswadi remained, the fever to fight blazing in his eyes.

"We are defenseless!" he shouted above the deafening symphony of destruction almost upon them.

"Maybe not," growled Bolan.

He darted from cover, calculating the approach of the nearest chopper in its hovering, roving manhunt. The death bird's weapons were temporarily silent, the crew's attention still focused on a point away from Bolan, where the chopper had shredded two *mujahedeen* guerrillas shouldering a wounded fighter from the killground.

The dust was clearing where blitzing cannon fire and riced the men into tiny pieces. The Huey banked around in search of more game, then hovered into a position Bolan had been waiting for.

He quick-footed to a grenade launcher that lay near the shattered, unrecognizable remains of the *mujahedeen* fighter responsible for taking out the enemy chopper moments earlier. The man had had enough time to prime the launcher before cannon fire ripped him apart, the tote-bag ammo pack with additional grenades on the ground near the discarded launcher.

Bolan raised the riflelike launcher, tracking toward the nearest Huey, steadying himself, feet planted wide, calculating windage and range as his finger curved around the trigger. He bucked into the recoil, the report lost beneath the cacophony of destruction around him.

He retrieved the tote pack, glanced inside and saw two remaining grenades at the instant another fireball flared in the night sky. He looked up from fitting another grenade into the launcher.

The fiery remains of a gunship plummeted down, well away from the surviving guerrillas, the blazing pieces of the shattered helicopter hurtling to earth and illuminating the desert night.

Bolan heard a spontaneous cheer go up from the freedom fighters, then he saw Karim Aswadi dash from the rocks and Jack, in search of medical help.

Bolan fought the impulse to return and check on his wounded buddy. The Executioner knew that would draw fire from the final Huey chopper banking around for a strafing run specifically aimed at him, the flames of the downed gunships making him an easy target.

He crouched low, ready.

The Huey was closing in from several hundred yards out, miniguns pounding on full-auto at the weaving, loose-limbed human target who suddenly dived beyond the streaming geysers of rapid-fire ricochets.

The evasive maneuver of the dark-clad figure surprised the pilot of the government chopper at the last possible instant as whamming projectiles spanged across the rocky ground fractions of an inch from the big man's heels.

Captain Baqir, the pilot at the controls of the Huey, ceased firing when his target's extraordinary dive from oncoming death took him momentarily out of the line of vision.

Baqir tugged the joystick between his legs in the cockpit.

The gunship responded with a sharp tilt, tossing some of the crew behind Baqir off balance. They stumbled and cursed the pilot, but the tactic saved the gunship when the man triggered his grenade launcher, the explosive narrowly missing the Plexiglas bubble through which Baqir again caught sight of the gunner on the ground.

The crewmen of the Huey saw the man trying to take out their gunship with his grenade launcher, and they understood.

The soldier at the mounted heavy machine gun in the hatchway thundered off a burst that dotted the ground where the figure below had stood when he fired his near miss seconds ago, but the target became most difficult, zigzagging around beneath the gunship's blind side again, feeding another grenade into the launcher.

Captain Baqir saw the man again.

Larger than the *mujahedeen*, thought Baqir. The American, Bolan! Baqir had been briefed by Major Kravak.

The pilot tried not to consider his own fate when he reported to Kravak and General Mahmoud the loss of two gunships and his failure to kill this elusive devil, Bolan, who required far more ammunition and time than tonight's timetable allowed.

Baqir knew he must return to the base commanded by Mahmoud and rearm before commencing phase two of tonight's action: the strafing flights over the Lavizan barracks, softening it for the assault within two hours of Mahmoud's forces. Baqir knew the risk, but he knew, too, that his training and loyalty to Mahmoud will pay off. Baqir would become General Baqir as promised, but first he had to kill the infidel, Bolan!

Baqir blinked in surprise at the speed with which the American fighting man on the ground reloaded the grenade launcher to track again at the hovering Huey. The pilot grinned when he saw the warrior down there toss aside the ammo pouch. Baqir knew that Bolan was now aiming his last grenade.

The pilot tugged up the gunship sharp and hard, desperately trying to maneuver the chopper out of range.

The American soldier on the ground responded to the evasive tactic, triggering the launcher before the gunship could gain altitude.

Baqir, USAF-trained legend-without-peer in the mostly lackluster government air force—Mahmoud's influence alone kept Baqir from the Iraqi front—goosed the Huey into another sharp zag.

Through the whirling fury, Baqir saw the flash of the grenade launcher, and the pilot's heart skipped a beat when the hurtling grenade arced through airspace where Baqir's gunship had hovered a millisecond earlier, missing the Huey.

I've got him!

Baqir grinned, throttling his copter around until Mack Bolan appeared, centered in the infrared target-acquisition system in Baqir's helmet. He clearly saw Bolan toss the grenade launcher away with one hand, swiveling around an assault rifle Bolan wore shoulder strapped.

For a fleeting second, Baqir stared in wonderment at this American, a man without a country, refusing to accept inevitable defeat, every inch the awesome human fighting machine Baqir had expected.

Captain Baqir navigated his gunship to stationary hover. The fighter pilot registered the crystallized infrared perception of Target Bolan.

The Executioner held his fire, realizing the inadequacy of even the assault rifle at the range of the hovering copter.

Baqir experienced only sadness. He concentrated on nothing else, in his gunship or on the ground or in the sky around him, except for a target in the sighting scope looking for cover and finding none.

The death of The Executioner will assure the gratitude of General Mahmoud; the glory of this kill will take me to the top!

Pilot Baqir confidently tightened on the trigger to open fire on a target he could not possibly miss.

14

Bolan had long lived his life knowing violent death would end everything for him at any second. There could be no other fate for a hellgrounder who lived life large the way Bolan did and in truth, Bolan would have it no other way.

It amazed him sometimes that he had continued to outfox and sidestep the inevitable for as long as he had through the bloody miles of his adult life.

At this instant it looked as if the sidestepping would not get it. The inevitable had come.

The Huey gunship hovered well beyond range of Bolan's AK-47. He knew the pilot of that chopper would have his thumb pressing toward a trigger. A damn good Iranian air-force pilot would be Bolan's executioner.

Bolan started a dodging, darting run toward high-ground cover he did not expect to reach, but he had nothing else.

Karim Aswadi appeared on a rocky slope close beneath the hovering Huey.

Aswadi took fast aim with a loaded grenade launcher, and a report like a popped paper bag in the wide open hills gave way in the next moment to an ear-splitting powerhouse blowup when the grenade caught the third Huey in the instant before the pilot of the Huey opened fire on Bolan.

Bolan spun into a combat crouch, AK-47 tracking around when he saw the plummeting fireball remains of Aswadi's bull's-eye.

A hush, absolute except for the crackling flames from the downed choppers, descended in sharp contrast to the pounding of battle. For a moment a shrill ringing clanged in Bolan's ears despite the plugs he wore, his heart bass-drumming against his rib cage.

The two warriors approached each other while around them the surviving freedom fighters regrouped, edgy eyes watching the sky for more choppers as they counted their losses.

Bolan and Aswadi angled abreast of each other toward the spot where they had left Grimaldi.

"I owe you, Karim," said Bolan. "Thanks for the fast work."

Aswadi appeared not to hear.

They strode past shredded bodies, torn and bleeding, scattered over the rocky ground. The two men could not miss the stunned muteness of survivors as postcombat shock set in when they saw what had happened to their friends and families.

"If I but knew with certainty what I suspect," Aswadi growled, "I would have let the pilot fire."

"You're wrong if you think the woman I brought into your camp called in those choppers," Bolan argued. The Executioner knew he had to go to Grimaldi, but he needed the trust of Aswadi for this Iranian hit to stand any chance at all of success. "Karim, there is no enemy ground force, remember? The army doesn't move this far away from Teheran after dark, which is why you're here. Your sentries would have spotted troop movement. Those choppers had coordinates on us."

Aswadi paused.

"Why do you defend the woman? You are unsettlingly sympathetic to your enemy."

"The truth matters," Bolan growled. "Mezhabi told them where the Hueys would find your base camp, probably when he passed word about your group importing me."

Aswadi glanced at the smoldering hulks of the downed gunships.

"Iranian air force. Is it possible Mezhabi informed for both General Mahmoud and Khomeini's people, or does this mean something more?"

Bolan forged ahead. "I figure it means we've got less time than we thought," he said. "We have to reach an understanding of trust now, Karim. Forget about Mezhabi as you have about whoever killed him. We have to reach Teheran and the Lavizan barracks. We have a chance unless Mahmoud is there already."

"I follow your reasoning," Aswadi said. "These gunships...Mahmoud strikes tonight, as the Russian woman said, but I hesitate to trust word from the enemy's mouth. The absurd charade of proposing an alliance; only a diversion to relax our defenses on the actual eve of take-over." Aswadi chuckled without humor. "Which supports your supposition of Mahmoud striking tonight. It would seem I must agree."

"Another reason I don't think we have to worry about Tanya," said Bolan, "although I've, ah, been wrong about the lady before. Look at it her way. The Soviets and Mahmoud knew we had Tanya in this camp. They attacked anyway because they wanted you out of the way before they took power. Tanya hasn't been gone long enough to get so far she could avoid hearing what happened here, and she'll realize the people she works for don't give a damn if they kill her. You're her enemy, Karim, but you treated her decently. If she does survive on her own in the hills tonight, she'll be out for blood, but it won't be yours."

A freedom fighter approached on the run to address Aswadi in staccato Farsi, to which Karim issued orders. The man snapped a field salute and hurried back toward the survivors of the attack.

Aswadi turned to Bolan.

"We have lost more than half our men. I pray to Allah you are true in your thinking, American. I believed eliciting your help in our struggle would insure victory. Will you be responsible for our destruction?''

"Time, Karim. We have no damn time.''

"You have traveled far and risked your life for us,'' Aswadi decided. "The men we need for the assault in Teheran are ready to leave at once. Those remaining shall assist dependents and wounded to the refugee camp. I only hope seven of us are sufficient to assault the operation we suspect at Lavizan barracks. If it is the core of Khomeini's security, it will be heavily guarded, though the barracks will appear deserted.''

"That's why you and your men are backup,'' Bolan told the *mujahedeen* leader. "I'm going into Khomeini's operation alone.''

"Impossible! You will be killed!''

"Not if Mahmoud is stirring the pot like we think he is; not if you're stirring Mahmoud and the Russians. I work best alone, Karim.'' Bolan thought of Strakhov. "And I could encounter an old friend tonight. I don't want anyone in the way when we tangle.'' He resumed striding toward Grimaldi.

"Get your men together to pull out with us immediately. I'll say goodbye to Jack.''

"We have three physicians in our unit,'' Aswadi replied, turning to hurry toward his men. "We have several wounded, but one of our doctors is with your friend now. It is too early to say of course, but your friend Grimaldi...may not make it. I'm sorry.''

WHEN GRIMALDI REGAINED a semblance of consciousness, the first thing he managed to mumble through the waves of pain could not be understood by the Iranian women in black veils and shawls who knelt to either side of him in a tent.

They were applying a dressing to his wounded leg, which had been straightened in a splint, he vaguely noted, while one of the women went in search of a translator. The other gestured, offering him round Iranian bread and melon, which Grimaldi refused with a faint head shake.

He gasped sharply as the gesture sent white-heat agony through him like sandpaper against exposed nerve ends. Grimaldi fought to stay conscious, wondering just how much of a chance he had of seeing tomorrow.

A guerrilla stuck his head inside the tent.

"Mr. Grimaldi, I regret to say we have exhausted our supply of pain killers."

Jack recognized the guy as one of the medics in Karim Aswadi's *mujahedeen* group.

"Wouldn't take 'em anyway," Grimaldi rasped through his pain, "and you've got lousy bedside manner, doc. Where's my friend? For that matter, where the hell am I?"

"In the refugee camp," the medic replied. "We sustained heavy losses, which is why our supplies of medication dwindle. Your friend and Karim and five others have gone into Teheran."

"And I should be with him!" Grimaldi growled

to himself, clenching fists in frustrated anger at his side, setting off another tremor of pain.

"You are most lucky to have survived until now," said the physician. "You perhaps do not appreciate the severity of your injuries."

"So why don't you tell me," Grimaldi rasped. "I remember being upended and hauled to cover, then...I lost it and here I am...feeling like I've been chewed by a bear and spit off a cliff. Damn! I hurt." He squinted, pain blurring his vision. He knew they had injected him with a strong sedative while he was unconscious. As the dope wore off the pain brought him awake. Now Grimaldi realized the pain would only intensify, and when unconsciousness came again it could be forever. "What...are my chances?" Grimaldi forced himself to ask, wondering why he was not aware of his own voice.

"Not good," the medic replied soberly. "By daylight I will lack even the bare necessities to stave off infection. You require immediate hospitalization, Mr. Grimaldi."

"And I'm another crummy statistic, huh, doc?"

The medic smiled grimly.

"With your spirit, Mr. Grimaldi, perhaps not. It is hoped the man Bolan can return quickly enough from Teheran, if their mission into the city—"

"Not *if*, doc..." Grimaldi forced himself to

rasp. Fight the pain. Fight the frigging pain! "With Bolan...it's *when*."

"The man does have a stunning capacity for turning disadvantage into advantage," the doctor conceded. "But you must excuse me now. There are others—"

"Of course." Grimaldi could barely whisper. He concentrated fully on grabbing on to the lucidity he felt being gnawed away by wavering emptiness erasing the edges of his vision. "Thanks...."

"May Allah spare you, Mr. Grimaldi. You have fought bravely for His cause."

The medic disappeared.

Grimaldi lowered his head back to the ground, hardly aware of the tent or the buzzing of insects drawn by the nearness of death. The veiled women of the *mujahedeen* and everything else seemed to sink into a haziness that was closing in from the periphery of his senses, devouring his consciousness.

This realization jolted Grimaldi with a fear like none he had ever known during his battle years with Mack Bolan.

Deliriously, obscure images kept filtering in and out of his senses, and Grimaldi thought of the days when he had returned fresh—make that sour—from two tours of combat flight duty in Nam. Then, he had found every hoped-for door to gainful employment slammed in his face. There had been accusing glares from peaceniks as if he was a baby killer and worse, when in truth he'd almost died more than once trying to keep the baby killers at bay before they swept across Southeast Asia like a red tide.

Grimaldi's fading consciousness grasped at memories of those days like a drowning man clawing desperately for a life raft; what remained of lucid thought through the pain told him that when thought died, it meant the end of him. . . .

The delirious American on the desolate Iranian ground reflected on Bolan and what he owed the big guy.

Grimaldi owed his life to the Executioner and not only from those times when Bolan had pulled Grimaldi's bacon from the grease in battle. Sure there had been those times, and Grimaldi had felt privileged to return the favor more than once during the missions when Jack flew Bolan and provided air cover. Beyond that, though, Grimaldi knew he would owe Big Guy Bolan until his dying breath.

When the veteran Nam pilot had been unable to find work on his return home, an uncle offered Grimaldi a gig flying some "execs" in and out of Vegas. Even after Jack got hip to the fact that his uncle, not to mention the "execs," worked for the Mafia, Grimaldi had not let it bother him much. He had had no real contact with hoodlums, the killers, heroin pushers and pimps chipping away at a great nation from within like a rotting, unstoppable cancer.

The Executioner had blitzed the operation that Grimaldi was flying for, and Grimaldi knew that by all rights the Man From Blood should have iced the pilot along with the hoods Jack saw Bolan blow away. It had been an audaciously wild-ass Executioner strike, but Nam-vet Bolan had sensed something in Grimaldi, maybe a kindred spirit gone wrong, and the Executioner had spared Jack.

Bolan had wised up Grimaldi, and in Bolan, Grimaldi had seen a smidgen of his own potential for the Right Way. From that moment on Jack had served as Bolan's pilot and combat support, their hellgrounding together spanning Bolan's war against the Mafia, the Executioner's stint for the government and Bolan's recent outlaw missions against the KGB and Major General Greb Strakhov in particular.

Grimaldi realized that these images of his life, flashing before his eyes remained as only the last, faint flickers of a dying candle, a sliver of light against a smothering pool of Stygian gloom creeping in from all sides. Grimaldi fought to hold on to even that, living, he knew, only in his mind and that ready to go, too.

Grimaldi had always considered himself an optimist, almost too much sometimes, but now as the spreading murk of unconsciousness swallowed him, he heard a calm little voice somewhere inside his head telling him to relax, to accept the inevitable because he had reached the end.

Grimaldi began to slide into unconsciousness, not accepting one damn bit of it, fighting it all the way, inevitable or not.

Final fleeting flashes swept over him: Bolan attacking what could be the heart of Khomeini's power; an Executioner taking on impossible odds against a would-be dictator, Mahmoud, and his gangsters; control of this war-torn country to the victor unless the Ayatollah's forces sliced their own cut of tonight's action.

And Grimaldi could only pray to God that his friend returned in time to keep Mrs. Grimaldi's little boy, Jack, from buying the farm in this refugee camp somewhere in godforsaken Iran.

Grimaldi, backsliding Catholic at the best of times, prayed to God for a world gone mad.

Grimaldi slid off the edge into unconsciousness, his soul screaming protest as the darkness swallowed him.

Don't let me die!

No!

No.

No. . . .

15

Rashad Hashem, a lieutenant in the army of the Islamic Republic, knocked briskly on Colonel Rafu's office door in the nether region of a deserted wing of the Lavizan barracks in northeast Teheran.

The sprawling, supposedly deserted complex gave Lieutenant Hashem a foreboding chill, first felt during the preceding week when Hashem's security force had received orders to remain at the barracks on twenty-four-hour standby alert. The call had been in response to the intel tremors of a *mujahedeen* plot to assassinate the Ayatollah.

The eerie, looming barracks buildings bespoke unworldly echoes to a soul sensitive to such things: too many atrocities committed here too recently for Rashad's liking, to say the least.

Hashem longed for the prerevolutionary days, when his most pressing concern would be no more than a sheep strayed from his flock; the days before this ominous premonition when there had been no reason for his gut to be tight, his throat parched, his fingers somehow restless near his Tokarev pistol.

Hashem heard Rafu's brusque command to enter. The security officer of this top-secret operation working out of Lavizan barracks stepped into the office, mentally debating whether or not to mention his premonition to his commanding officer.

Rafu, an animal-featured hulk of a man who reminded Hashem of an ape in uniform, glared up from shuffling a handful of manila folders into a briefcase.

Rafu stood from his chair behind the metal desk, the lone pieces of furniture in the stuffy, windowless office. He snapped shut the briefcase.

"This is the last of what I will be taking with us, Lieutenant. All is in readiness?"

Hashem decided not to mention his premonition. He would be gone from this place within minutes, Allah willing. Perhaps, thought Hashem, I will see home again after all.

"The convoy is ready and awaits your order to leave, Colonel."

Rafu purred, a peculiarly feline sound from a man who looked like an ape.

"Very good. The cabinet of files, the tools of our dear plastic-surgeon friend, Dr. LeQueux... and what of...the subject?"

"He will travel in the second vehicle with two of my men for protection." Hashem wondered why Rafu queried him on matters already well discussed earlier, after the decision came to relocate.

Colonel Rafu looked distinctly on edge, Hashem decided, the way Rashad felt. "You and I shall ride in the lead car with three of my men," he reminded the colonel. "A fourth vehicle with more of my soldiers will complete the convoy. Dr. LeQueux will ride with us. The facilities in Firuzkuh have been prepared. We should reach there before dawn."

Rafu purred again.

"You have done your job well, Lieutenant. Your—"

The colonel interrupted himself, something Hashem had never seen him do. Both men turned to a sliding-panel portion of the shabby office wall that whispered open to reveal a hidden entrance Hashem had not known about.

A man stood in the half-light just inside the hidden doorway and Hashem discerned an aura of pure evil emanating from the black-robed, black-turbaned figure. The wispy beard and pallid features of the gaunt ancient standing there reminded Rashad of a dead man. Hashem knew with a certainty that he had never encountered this being before during the months Rafu had operated this covert security operation.

Ayatollah Khomeini.

The real Khomeini, Hashem wondered.

His duties had not included a need to know concerning the detailed workings of Rafu's operation. Hashem only knew it involved a deception using elderly men with physical builds similar to the

Ayatollah, their features altered by Dr. LeQueux to match Iran's spiritual and political ruler.

Hashem appreciated that such knowledge could get him killed and so had been most satisfied knowing only what Rafu considered pertinent to Hashem's providing security there at the headquarters of the operation.

Rafu, meanwhile, oversaw security on rare public appearances by the "Ayatollah" on government-controlled television and at religious ceremonial rallies, such as the one yesterday.

As he gazed upon the unforgettable presence in the shadows, Lieutenant Hashem found great comfort in knowing he had not been briefed on any of the events of the "assassination" of the day before; he knew of it at all only because one of the Ayatollah's human duplicates disappeared unaccountably and Dr. LeQueux had put in another of his rare appearances at Lavizan.

Colonel Rafu had been particularly edgy ever since the double-agent informer, Mezhabi, told someone in Intel that Karim Aswadi's people had imported a man known as The Executioner, a "penetration specialist." Mezhabi subsequently leaked word that General Mahmoud, of the Ayatollah's supposedly loyal army, intended to strike these barracks this very night.

Hashem regained his lapsed sense of the moment; the statuelike figure, standing with arms crossed, commanding his attention.

Rafu cleared his throat.

"You may leave us now, Lieutenant. Have your drivers start their engines. We leave when I join up with you within a few minutes. That will be all."

"As you wish, my Colonel."

Hashem gladly withdrew, leaving Rafu alone with the man, the *presence*, in the secret doorway.

Hashem hurried through the dark, extended, echoing halls of the deserted barracks, imagining eyes watching from everywhere in the surrounding darkness, making him hurry to get to his men, the convoy; to be gone from there.

The lieutenant's premonition would not leave him, nor would uncertainties about Death stalking this treacherous Teheran night.

He would bestow copious thanks to Allah the minute the convoy arrived safely at the new headquarters for Colonel Rafu's operation in Firuzkuh. The town was not far from Teheran and suited Rafu and those few he served who knew of this operation.

The move suited the security officer assigned to protect the colonel's operation. Lieutenant Hashem had advised relocating much earlier, stating the difficulties inherent in protecting the sprawling Lavizan complex while maintaining absolute secrecy so as not to draw attention to Rafu's operation, but Rafu had remained adamant that his operation be based in the nation's capital. It had taken warning of a possible attack by Mahmoud's rebel army force to persuade Rafu to move at this last minute to Firuzkuh.

Last minute, Lieutenant Hashem thought worriedly.

He hurried toward a doorway that led out of the barracks building to the waiting convoy. He felt the sense of foreboding, a sense of doom, stronger than before. The lieutenant told himself that if he never saw his home again, it would be because of whatever happened to him within the next few short minutes before they left there.

It all depended—and *all*, Hashem knew, meant his own life, his very existence—on whether or not one or both man killers chose to attack the Lavizan barracks tonight; two enemies who would have no qualms whatever about defacing these barracks with glistening, dripping blood again.

16

The Executioner crouched in deep shadow thirty yards from the convoy of four unmarked vehicles. They were parked in readiness to depart this sector of the dark Lavizan barracks.

Bolan had donned his night combat blacksuit.

A black cosmetic smeared on his face completed the nighttime effect, making the Executioner just another shadow in the postmidnight quiet of sleeping Teheran.

The Beretta 93-R nestled in its elongated holster under his left arm. Big Thunder rode in quick-draw leather strapped Old West gunfighter style to his right hip. He carried extra clips for both weapons on a combat harness, along with strangulation gear, grenades, a Fairbairon-Sykes knife and a new head weapon for his quiet penetration of the Lavizan barracks. The nightstalker knew the "quiet" hit could go "loud" within seconds if Karim Aswadi and his men opened on the numbers, at which point Bolan anticipated ample use of the combat weapon borrowed from one of Aswadi's guerrillas: a 9mm Uzi submachine gun, a nasty room-broom favorite of the warring factions in the Mideast and most other parts of the world.

Boasting two 32-round magazines welded together at right angles, the diminutive SMG could fire six hundred parabellum flesh eaters per minute. The scaled-down stutter gun could empty a magazine in three seconds. Bolan carried extra magazines in his battle harness.

The barracks' atmosphere of solitude belied the secretive activity Bolan observed.

He sensed apprehension underpinning this waiting convoy bathed in the light of a crisp silver moon.

He counted and placed what men he could see, knowing there would be more in one of the looming, supposedly deserted buildings that reminded him of his old basic-training stomping grounds at Fort Benning. But first he would have to deal with these human targets in and around the vehicles; *deal* as in *kill*, and it would be no cakewalk even for a specialist in this dirty business.

He counted thirteen rifle-toting Iranian soldiers; six in and around the last vehicle in the line; three at the first vehicle where another man stood, not a soldier, impatiently smoking a cigarette; two in the cab of a truck and, most interesting to Bolan, two especially alert soldiers scanning the night from either side of a limousine with tinted windows.

Bolan frowned. The commander and his security officer would ride in the lead vehicle, a limo with tinted windows. Bolan wondered about the limo and the civilian waiting by the lead car.

He focused particular attention on the guy while he digested the rest of it, formulating the strike.

The civilian waiting near the officer's car at the front of the convoy had classically chiseled Gallic features, eccentrically coiffed silver hair, worn long. He looked like a glossy magazine ad for an exclusive Paris tailor.

Bolan placed him: Gerard LeQueux, the best plastic surgeon on the Continent.

Bolan recalled the bad doctor's dossier from his Mafia files.

LeQueux sold his services to only the highest bidders and right here, right now, in Teheran, that could only mean Khomeini.

Bolan glanced at the luminous dials of his wristwatch.

Twenty seconds and the killing would begin.

Twenty seconds and Karim Aswadi's *mujahedeen* fighters would attack General Mahmoud's forces, deployed by the rebel army officer and his GRU advisor across rooftops and in alleys of the lower-class residential structures adjacent to the southeast corner of the Lavizan complex. Bolan had judged the alleys to be farthest from any of the thoroughfares near the compound's stormfence perimeter.

When Bolan, Aswadi and the five fighters of the *mujahedeen* guerrilla unit arrived in the vicinity of the barracks, the compound had appeared as forlorn as a supposedly unused military facility possibly could.

Bolan had first taken advantage of Aswadi's relinquishing command of the operation by guiding the guerrillas on an ultrasoft reconnaissance of the slumbering neighborhood.

With no sign of Mahmoud's rebels within the perimeter of the barracks, Bolan figured either the notion of Mahmoud striking there tonight had been off base, or the idea of a Khomeini "double" operation based in these barracks had been erroneous, or both.

Or the plotting Mahmoud and his GRU backup had arrived, aware an Executioner strike on these same barracks to be likely, and Mahmoud had chosen to bide his time; to wait until Bolan and the *mujahedeen* showed before snapping the trap to wipe out Aswadi and the Khomeini deal in one hard punch.

Karim's guerrillas needed no pointers in soundless prowling, years of waging guerrilla warfare serving them well, but to a man they looked to the imported American specialist when they found what they were looking for.

Mahmoud had been sharp enough to spot the same weak point in the barracks perimeter and had deployed fifteen of his men among the shadows of a block of one-level adobe residences.

Bolan and the Iranian freedom fighters crouched on a roof, a two-level commercial structure closed at this hour. Their position allowed the Executioner's team to discern soldiers armed with AK-47s, keenly eyeballing the compound across an open stretch of dusty ground, waiting silent and ready for the appearance of Bolan and company to strike the barracks; waiting for Mahmoud to give the order to close the trap.

Bolan was sure that none of Mahmoud's force realized they were outflanked, their trap ready to spring the wrong way, back on them.

Aswadi quietly pointed out Mahmoud, who stood back from his men.

"The man with him beside the car is Major Kravak," Aswadi whispered to Bolan. "GRU."

Bolan frowned.

No sign of Strakhov.

The Executioner parted company with Aswadi and the commandos after indicating the best deployment for engaging Mahmoud's force.

Bolan soft-probed the barracks' perimeter. He and the *mujahedeen* synchronized watches before the nightstalker in blacksuit disappeared into the early-morning gloom.

Aswadi and his men split up to prepare their part of the attack.

Bolan penetrated the complex easily enough, practically under the noses of Mahmoud's watching, waiting rebel infantrymen, none of whom detected the subtle shift of night when the dark-clad nightfighter melded as one with the elements and negotiated the chain link fence. It was child's play after some of the joints Bolan had busted into, though he did not ignore the lack of visible evidence of sentries and the impression of little or no security about this place.

He continued deeper into the maze of two-level barracks buildings, probing around the elongated structures that were separated by walkways and parking areas, cloaked in isolation.

He moved silently and with economy of motion, clutching the Uzi in close, doing his best to digest the layout, ever mindful of the passing seconds, the falling numbers.

He hoped Karim and his fighters met no interference in the delicate maneuver of outflanking Mahmoud's small force.

Bolan had sectored off half the barracks area in less than the time allotted, after which the *mujahedeen* could launch their ambush outside the perimeter.

He continued deeper into the labyrinth of barracks.

Bolan found himself considering the probability of the real target, Khomeini's operation, not being there at all or already gone, Mahmoud and his GRU man intending to salvage what they could and take out the *mujahedeen* and Bolan.

Especially Bolan, if King Cannibal Strakhov was on deck.

Bolan suspected the KGB chief would give his life to take out The Executioner.

Bolan found the convoy in front of a barracks building blocked from view of any point beyond the perimeter.

Bolan spent part of the remaining minute before Aswadi's scheduled opening fire, eyeing the building behind the convoy.

The structure looked dark and forlorn as the rest.

Bolan disregarded this impression, knowing he would find the commander of the operation inside the building.

The convoy appeared ready to pull out, waiting for some final business transacted by the officers inside the seemingly uninhabited barracks.

Another glance at his watch.

Five seconds.

He shifted his attention and the Uzi back to the four vehicles, the thirteen infantrymen and especially the limo with the tinted windows.

In the clarity of ascending combat consciousness he ticked off the final numbers into the attack, disciplining into his subconscious the troubles threatening to distract him from the dirty work he had to do.

Grimaldi.

Bolan would not consider the unthinkable, that his hellground pal could already be dead in that secret refugee camp.

The Executioner had to stay alive and wind up this Teheran wipeout, then *maybe* Grimaldi had a chance if Bolan could get them out of Iran to a hospital in time....

Tanya.

Where the hell is she? *Who* and *what* the hell was this woman he cared about?

He could not get the tough, yet somehow vulnerable, beautiful blonde out of his mind, and he knew this could be his deadliest mistake.

Mahmoud.

A power-grabbing savage with too much blood on his hands, ready to take a bath in the stuff tonight if it got him control.

And Strakhov.

Target number one.

Would Bolan find the boss KGB mobster in Teheran this night of blood?

The numbers ticked to zero.

The *crack* of rifle fire punctured the night from outside the perimeter of the barracks.

And on the moonlit tarmac where Bolan and his Uzi had bided their time, the Executioner went to work.

17

The gunfire had the intended effect. Bolan had held his fire on the convoy, counting on Aswadi's *mujahedeen* fighters to engage Mahmoud's rebel strike force and divert the attention of the Iranian combat troopers assigned to protect the four vehicles on the tarmac.

The riflemen in the rear vehicle of the convoy scrambled to join the two already positioned to either side of the unmarked limousine with the tinted windows.

The eight soldiers crouched, rifles ready, backs to the limo in tight defensive posture around it.

Two soldiers next to the truck in front of the limo briskly fanned out with the three riflemen near the lead car, the five heading in the direction of the nearby gunfire to investigate, leaving plastic surgeon LeQueux decidedly distressed by these unexpected events.

The automatic weapons' fire from beyond the perimeter intensified.

The Executioner triggered the Uzi, dousing the

five soldiers in front with a prolonged figure-eight stitching, toppling the five under a blazing sheet of 9mm death.

He reloaded on the run, his movement an almost indiscernible shifting of the night, nothing more. He ran as fast as he could to the other side of the limo, skirting the corpse-strewed ground near the front, where fresh corpses were still twitching in the moonlight.

The troops maintained a close-in defense around the limo. They opened a thundering AK-47 salvo at the spot where Bolan's Uzi had flashed.

Bolan pelted past the front limo where LeQueux cowered like a confused rat, not knowing which way to bolt.

Bolan shifted the Uzi to his left fist and unholstered the Beretta 93-R. Without slowing he pegged off a parabellum tab to a cannibal more dangerous than those he served because scum like LeQueux kept to the background and took their cut when the killing had finished.

Until now.

LeQueux never saw his Executioner. The Rembrandt of plastic surgery spray-painted the car behind him with a ghastly mural of blood and brains when the Beretta's slug cored the Frenchman's left eye and burst away the back of his skull, the impact pasting LeQueux to the limo; legs buckled and he slid to the ground, into hell.

The soldiers around the other limo continued

pouring deafening autofire at the spot where the Uzi's flashes had knifed seconds ago.

The Executioner closed in on them undetected, the 93-R reholstered, the Beretta equipped with a sound suppressor and flash hider for night firing.

He passed the truck between the lead car and the next limo, priming a grenade on his run that took him several feet within the hard guys' position.

Bolan fast-balled the grenade, covering as much distance as he could, hotfooting away from the limo.

He propelled himself into a dive, hugging the ground.

The sharp detonation of the grenade banged behind him.

He twisted onto his back in time to see three of the riflemen nearest him pitch forward, tossed by the force of the blast, the soldier in the middle missing most of his head, the other two dazed.

Bolan canceled the two with a lethal stutter from the Uzi and the dazed became dead.

The nightstriker moved low in double time, away from these Uzi flashes. He charged around the blocking hulk of the rear vehicle, picking out more targets as he moved.

Three crumpled bodies lay on the other side of the smoked-window limo, killed instantly from razoring shrapnel from the grenade.

The detonation echoed between the barracks buildings.

Two surviving soldiers alongside the limo struggled to recover their senses, one of the riflemen tracking on Bolan without knowing it.

The Executioner stayed under cover of night. He triggered a burst from the Uzi, red-hot parabellums pulping the rifleman's chest, red muck belching out of the soldier's back as he tumbled against the limo. The door was edging open, someone inside responding to the grenade blast.

The limo looked bullet and bomb-proof. The occupants did not know this or simply wanted out of this firefight to reach what they considered the safety of the nearest building.

The front passenger door of the vehicle nudged against the impacting weight of the falling man. The back door eased open, figures inside scrambling out.

The last Iranian soldier stared at death everywhere he looked, stunned because less than thirty seconds ago everything had seemed all right. He triggered a blast from his bucking AK-47, frantically hammering the night without a target.

Bolan closed in on the car from another angle, triggering the Uzi.

The projectiles ate out the hardguy's chest, back-flipping the bullet-riddled body across the hood of the car.

The rear door of the limo slammed shut.

The front door started to, the occupants obviously rethinking their escape.

Bolan triggered a stutter before the front door could close.

A gasp punctuated the *thwack* of slugs bursting open flesh. The door swung outward again, a dead body leaning half out of the car, half reclining from the front seat, spreading a pool of blood on the ground beneath.

Bolan dashed toward the car, rapidly reloading without a glance at the uniformed corpse half in, half out of the car like a grotesque jack-in-the-box.

An arm from inside the car reached across the body to grab the door handle and pull it shut.

Bolan triggered a 3-round burst, messily amputating at the wrist, the fingers of the severed hand remaining gripped around the door handle.

Bolan kicked the door wide open, activating an interior light, bringing the mortal panic in the limo into crisp focus.

A figure, face completely swathed in bandages, scrambled for escape out the opposite back door of the limo as the Man From Death loomed in for the kill.

The soldier in the front seat shrieked, bouncing and screaming, oblivious to anything except the throbbing stump of wrist and the stream of high-pressure red he tried unsuccessfully to stem with his remaining hand.

Bolan put this bodyguard out of his misery with a 9mm bullet.

The bandaged plastic-surgery patient in back managed to yank open his door and start out of the limo.

The Uzi yammered again, loud in the confines of the car, spewing slugs to help this one out of the car, blasting away spine and the back of his head into slimy chunks of blood.

Bolan straightened from leaning in the car, the haze of gun smoke in the confines of the limo irritating his eyes. The acrid stench of cordite assaulted his nostrils.

One minute had elapsed since Aswadi's guerrillas engaged Mahmoud's rebel force outside the perimeter, signaling this assault.

The banging of rifle fire in the distance continued, more sporadic than before.

Bolan hurried to the truck that was parked in front of the limo. He paused at the tailgate to pull back the tarp flaps.

He saw vague shapes: a file cabinet and padlocked crates in the dim truck bed; files for this complex operation, LeQueux's equipment, but no men. No reason to delay.

The Executioner hustled toward the closest barracks building, death on his mind and in his fist, not knowing what he would find.

As the brutal firefight raged too near for comfort, General Mahmoud heard the crack of a projectile whistle past his ear, barely missing him.

Mahmoud sought quick cover behind his disabled command car, scanning over the chassis, aiming his Tokarev pistol with two hands, hunting for the source of the near-fatal shot.

A rifle spoke from a nearby rooftop, and a heavy bullet hammered into the car's body.

The general fired at the muzzle-flash, rewarded by the clatter of a rifle dropping from the roof, followed a second later by the heavy thump of the man he killed.

Mahmoud held his position, keeping his head down, searching for the safest route of withdrawal, trying not to let panic make him careless. He knew he had no hope whatsoever now except to run; try to escape Iran alive.

He heard the exchange of fire between his men and the attacking force diminish into single reports back and forth.

Mahmoud's stunned mind whirled.

How did Khomeini learn of my plans?

Nothing had gone right since the man Bolan arrived in the country!

Mahmoud realized his carefully laid plans to grab power and deliver the Executioner's head stood no chance. Except for the few rebels trying to hold their positions in the nearby residences, Mahmoud knew most of his men were slain, cut down in the ambush.

When my dead are found, Khomeini will know and I shall be forced to join my men, Mahmoud thought.

He darted from his useless car.

The neighborhood remained dark, the frightened residents hiding in their unlit homes.

I can escape while they fight each other, Mahmoud decided. There is no one to stop me!

He sidestepped the body of Major Kravak. The GRU man had fallen from the car when the ambush surprised them less than a minute ago, a burst of gunfire flattening the front tires of Mahmoud's vehicles before tracking to riddle Kravak.

I have more of a chance on foot, Mahmoud assured himself.

He cut sharply toward an alley in a desperate effort to place as much distance as he could between himself and the fighting.

An AK-47-armed man wearing *mujahedeen* guerrilla garb emerged from the moon-splashed alleyway to stand firm, blocking Mahmoud's retreat.

Mahmoud froze several feet short of the guerrilla.

"Karim Aswadi," Mahmoud said without lowering his pistol. "I thought Khomeini—"

The guerrilla smiled grimly above the assault rifle that was trained unwaveringly at Mahmoud.

"Wrong, General. The Ayatollah cannot risk sending a backup force to counterattack, compromising his operation here."

Mahmoud could not conceal his surprise. He realized the gunfire had tapered off to nothing between his men and the ambushers, the battle done, his rebels dead or surrendered.

"I . . . heard gunfire from the barracks. Bolan?" he asked, scheming as he spoke, realizing he could salvage this, confident he could deceive this man Aswadi who, the general had heard, loathed the necessity of force.

Mahmoud started to relax, thinking of how easy it would be for a desert-law aggressor like himself to persuade a misguided pacifist.

"Ah, perhaps we could negotiate," he suggested, his fear gone, replaced by a cynical confidence. "My dear Aswadi, you would have much to gain if—"

Aswadi fired.

General Mahmoud ceased to exist.

18

An invisible Executioner in blacksuit stormed soundlessly into the dark, vacant-looking barracks.

The glass door sighed shut behind Bolan as if sealing him in the cryptlike silence of the hallway that stretched ahead into unfathomable gloom.

He jogged forward, Uzi ready, night vision adjusting to the smattering of moonlight from unshaded windows in the bay and noncom one-room units lining the corridor. The hallway extended along the length of the building. At the end of the hall Bolan discerned a stairway leading up.

He hustled along the hall, peering through open doorways, finding no one, nothing.

He heard no more shooting from the direction of Aswadi's battle with Mahmoud's group.

The night beyond the barracks buzzed, residents calling warily to one another, trying to decide if they should risk stepping from their homes to investigate the shooting. Barking dogs created a canine symphony.

Bolan halted when he got within ten feet of the bottom step of the stairway.

He heard someone hurrying down, light-footed but in too much of a hurry.

Bolan flattened himself to a wall, a suggestion of black against black, nothing more. He brought up the Uzi.

An Iranian army officer dashed from the stairway, oblivious of the Bolan presence, rushing toward a side door that looked out onto the tarmac where Bolan had massacred the convoy less than a moment ago.

Bolan eyeballed the scurrying figure: too young to be CO of Khomeini's operation at Lavizan barracks.

Bolan tabbed him as security officer—the bigwigs probably upstairs when Bolan hit the convoy—on his way to retrieve an emergency vehicle kept separate from the convoy for a contingency such as this.

The young officer appeared relieved and anxious to escape the fate of his men.

"Halt," Bolan ordered quietly in Farsi, one of the few words he knew of the language.

He intended to make fast work of persuading this security officer to divulge information.

The Iranian twirled to the side, away from the command, drawing the holstered pistol from his hip.

Bolan regrettably triggered the Uzi.

And nothing happened.

He tossed the jammed weapon, flinging himself sideways, clawing for the Beretta.

He stared into the frightened eyes of the officer who did not realize he was looking into the eyes of Death.

Bolan held his fire as the Iranian had, watching the guy cast one parting look at the gloom where a voice had commanded and nothing happened.

The soldier looked confused, relieved. He lowered his pistol and continued scurrying toward the door.

Bolan reached out and grabbed the man's collar the instant before he touched the door handle. Bolan yanked hard, depositing the man on the floor.

The Executioner pressed a knee down on the officer's chest, pinning him, shifting his fist from the collar to hold the soldier's head to the floor using a one-handed strangle clamp.

Bolan touched the snout of the silenced Beretta to the man's sweaty forehead.

"Name," he demanded in English, in a terse whisper.

"L—Lieutenant Hashem," croaked the soldier. The man shook with fear. "Please...do not kill me...."

"Who's upstairs?"

"Colonel Rafu and...*him*!"

"Khomeini?"

Hashem nodded, jittery.

"Who. . . are you?"

Bolan heard sirens wailing in the Teheran night. He figured Khomeini's local authorities were responding to the firefights in and near the Lavizan barracks, giving the Executioner only a few minutes, if that, for the grand slam of this wipeout of cannibals. Many things counted in a world of fighting, killing, dying for what mattered, and Bolan had to know something about this man before he went up those stairs for the big kill.

He did not move the snout of the Beretta from the forehead of this enemy, nor the strangle grip at Hashem's throat.

"Lieutenant, you heard me toss away the Uzi just now. Why didn't you fire at me when you had the chance?"

"I've. . . never killed," the frightened whisper choked. "They came. . . took us from our homes, our families. . . forced us to join. . . . Who are you?"

Bolan eased the Beretta away, keeping Hashem covered. He relieved the officer of his pistol, then released him and stepped back, gesturing to the side door that led out of the building.

"I'm your second chance, Lieutenant. Grow some wings and fly. Everything is changing tonight. Get to your family where you belong."

Hashem scrambled toward the exit, pausing to turn and stare at indiscernible speaking shadows, as if expecting a trick.

"You are. . . the Executioner?"

Bolan started toward the stairs.

"Scram, Lieutenant. I see you again tonight, I'll kill you."

Hashem gave up trying to see what he could not.

"You are Allah's mercy," he whispered after the silent, moving darkness. "And His judgment."

The young officer disappeared.

Bolan ascended into the pitch-black, three stairs at a time, holstering the Beretta.

The nightstriker unleathered Big Thunder.

He topped the landing and started left toward a rectangle of light spilling onto the hallway floor from an open door three down to his right.

At that precise moment, three briskly moving figures emerged in rapid succession into the corridor as if on prearranged cue to confront the nighthunter.

Bolan paused close enough to the periphery of light for the three to see the Executioner and the stainless-steel hand cannon tracking on them.

The blonde who called herself Tanya Yesilov emerged first from the lighted office doorway, pushed from behind by an ape in an Iranian army uniform.

Colonel Rafu propelled the woman roughly, his left fist filled with her hair, cruelly arching the woman's head back so she could barely see where he pushed her. The colonel had a Tokarev pistol pressed to her right temple.

The third figure followed Rafu into the rectangle of light in the corridor before realizing the Bolan presence.

The old, scraggle-whiskered, unhealthy-looking gent in the black robe and black turban sidestepped with an agility that belied his years, dodging to hide behind Rafu and their shield, the woman. The spry old-timer's eyes were sharp and crafty in the brutal countenance of Ayatollah Ruholla Khomeini.

Bolan triggered Big Thunder and the Ayatollah's head exploded into awful red, the decapitated corpse reeling to crumple in a corner like a sack of discarded laundry, the briefcase he carried skidding across the floor toward Bolan.

Rafu snaked a forearm under and around the woman in front of him, clamping the blonde against him in a deadly mugger's grip. His narrowed eyes on Bolan, Rafu applied pressure on the gun against the woman's temple.

Bolan tracked to them with the AutoMag before the headless body fountaining blood finished its fall.

The Executioner held his fire.

The woman watched him from her trapped position, her eyes as impossible to read as ever.

Rafu snickered from where he shielded himself.

"You will drop your weapon, please, or the woman will die."

Bolan snickered right back.

"What makes you think I give a damn?" Iced eyes and cold death in his fist aimed at the blonde and the cannibal hiding behind her. He nodded to the sack of garbage in the corner. "Just out of curiosity, Colonel, is this the real one or don't you know?"

The ape holding the woman and the gun did not move.

"That is something you will never know. Throw down your weapon, please. My captive and I are leaving. I know something about you, Mack Bolan. You will not murder this woman in cold blood, even if she is a KGB agent."

The AutoMag stayed leveled.

"Maybe you should know something about the lady, yourself," Bolan growled. "She's not KGB and you've got more trouble than you think, Colonel. My guess is CIA."

Rafu blinked in surprise.

The woman used that exact instant to unexpectedly, unceremoniously collapse. Her knees buckled, her shapely body wilted to the floor away from the hold around her throat.

Her dead-fall pulled Rafu's body forward, then the colonel released her to track his pistol on Bolan, realizing in the moment it took to recover from the surprise of Bolan's words and the blonde's faint that he stood exposed.

Bolan slammed off a round, the deafening report cannonading through the tomblike building.

Rafu's pistol flew from his hand, as did his fingers.

The wounded cannibal spun around with a shrill scream, falling to his knees, grabbing wildly at his red-bubbling, digitless stump.

Bolan stepped forward, straight-arming the .44 AutoMag, at the guy's disbelieving features.

The woman recovered from her "faint," scrambling from the line of fire.

From behind the mighty hand cannon, a graveyard voice demanded of Rafu, "Is this man the real Khomeini? It's finished, Colonel. LeQueux is dead, your soldiers are dead, the guy LeQueux worked on to replace whoever I killed yesterday at the pavilion." The Man From Ice nodded to the headless corpse in the corner. "The real one? Tell me, Colonel."

Rafu lifted an agony-quivering ape face to look into the AutoMag's muzzle.

"The Ayatollah...has been dead for two years." A strange quiet voice, almost as if forgetting blown-away fingers. "Those...I serve...to hold power, they need...a figurehead...I have failed...they...will kill me...."

"No, they won't," Bolan assured him.

He blew the guy's brains out.

Rafu's abruptly decapitated body flipped backward atop the other corpse in the corner.

Bolan picked up the briefcase that had dropped.

The banshee rise and fall of sirens in the night

sounded closer, coming in on the Lavizan barracks from more than one direction.

Git time.

He turned, the briefcase in one hand, fisting Big Thunder.

Right into the sights of Colonel Rafu's pistol, which a million-dollar blonde aimed at a spot directly between Bolan's eyes.

19

Bolan did not lower the AutoMag as he turned, aligning the .44 at the vicinity of the woman's navel.

"Looks like a Mexican standoff."

"Not if I can help it," the blonde answered evenly, listening to the approaching sirens. "I don't want to be caught here any more than you do."

"What do you want, Tanya?"

"That's not my name, as you seem to know. I want my Walther PPK, the one you took from me yesterday at General Mahmoud's when you killed Yuri Steranko, and I want to know how you know what you told Rafu."

"About you being CIA? Just a guess and I wasn't sure but it worked. That and your fainting spell."

"You believe what Rafu said?"

"About the Ayatollah already long dead? Yeah, I believe it. Rafu had no reason and too much pain to lie, and you people have been picking up the same whispers. This must fit in real well with the Company's plans for the region."

She nodded, not relaxing, her right index knuckle white around the trigger of the pistol she aimed at him.

"I was planted in Soviet government service years ago. My father was American, my mother Russian. They met and married in West Germany. My mother died giving birth to me. My father brought me to America as an infant. The... Company approached me when I was in Harvard, asking if I would return to the Soviet Union posing as a dissident, hoping the KGB would try to recruit me, as they did."

"How did you get here from Aswadi's camp?"

"My Iranian contact in Teheran knew I would be in Aswadi's camp and waited far enough away so the sentries would not see him. I knew what was happening here, you see. I was with Major Kravak when Mezhabi informed to him and General Mahmoud."

More sirens joined the first, closing in on the tableau of man and woman in the ghostly corridor of the barracks building.

"So the KGB sends what they think is a novice agent to play wifey window dressing for Steranko," Bolan summarized tersely, "not knowing their 'Ellie Talbot' is a CIA mole monitoring the Soviet presence in Iran."

"And how did you guess this?"

"Your Tanya had her American act down too well. The mastery of colloquialism—'the ball's in your court,' or just now, 'Mexican standoff'—the KGB could program that into you, but when I handcuffed you to that tree in Aswadi's camp... you got mad enough to claw my eyes out and you swore in English. You were supposed to be Russian; you should have cussed me in Russian.

"That's not much, maybe, but it's my experience when people really swear from the soul, they lapse into their mother tongue. Grimaldi did it tonight in Italian when he got hit. I never heard Jack speak Italian in the years I've known him."

"Jack...is he—"

"I don't know. I want to get out of here to find out, so let's not stand here and shoot each other. You've done a good job of trying to string me along already."

"My orders from the Company were...to exploit your presence here," she said. "Karim Aswadi is a good man. His moderates would restabilize Iran, the whole Mideast."

"Strakhov was the bait to hold me in case Aswadi and I had a falling out."

She nodded.

"After I escaped from the camp and saw the gunships and witnessed the attack, I was afraid you might be delayed, that Rafu would get away. I've had commando training. I came here in the hopes of stopping them. They stopped me. I, ah, hoped you would be along. I knew the lie about Strakhov being in Teheran would do it. I am sorry about that, but when I learned of what Rafu had here, I knew I had to do something. I needed your help. . . more than I thought. Thanks, big guy,'' she said genuinely from behind her pistol.

"The Company has a Terminate On Sight order on me to all agents," he reminded her, watching closely the knuckle of her trigger finger.

He did not want to kill this blonde, whoever she was, but if she twitched that trigger finger in the slightest, Bolan would have no choice but to dodge and fire.

"Time's over, lady. We're starting to look like statues."

She lowered her pistol.

"You've done too much for the good guys this time, Mack. And you just might kill me."

The approaching sirens entered the neighborhood streets adjacent to the barracks, whining toward the main gate several buildings away.

"There's a truck outside," Bolan told her. "I'm taking it from the convoy. I'll pass those Teheran cops, wave Rafu's authorization and be gone before they find this. It's a truckload of Rafu's files that Aswadi will make good use of. I can get you out, too."

"I can get myself out. Where is my gun?"

"The Walther? With Grimaldi. Come with me and get it yourself. Your KGB bosses may suspect who you are. That could be why Kravak let Mahmoud attack Aswadi's camp when they knew you were there."

"It's a chance I have to take," the lady told him. "There's too much at stake...the suffering I saw in the camp tonight, the human misery...I've got to feel I'm doing something about that."

She stepped forward and melded her body to Bolan's, feathery fingertips twining at the back of his neck to draw his face to hers for a kiss; a warm, vibrant living thing of need and promise, her body curving in all the right places, pressing against him. Then she broke the kiss and he let her go.

The sirens outside became louder as vehicles closed in on the Lavizan compound through the main gate.

She turned and darted back through the lighted doorway of Rafu's office.

Bolan reached the door after her in time to see her disappear beyond a sliding wall panel in the nearest partition of the windowless window.

The panel snapped shut, leaving not a trace of its presence and no indication of how it activated, though Bolan knew it would work only from the other side.

Inwardly he cursed headstrong blondes everywhere, especially million-dollar ones belonging to the wrong side who touched a warrior's soul just long enough to make the real pain come alive again; the truth that what a man needs to stay mentally and spiritually alive, a good woman to share and build and dream with, something that could never be his.

She reminded him of April.

And he did not know her name.

He hustled from the office with the appropriated briefcase, heading down the stairs toward the truck in the convoy, knowing he would make it to the truck, to rejoin Aswadi for withdrawal from Teheran to the secret camp where the *mujahedeen* guerrillas awaited them.

The soundless black shadows shifted. The left door of the truck cab opened.

Bolan withdrew a chemically treated tissue from a slit pocket of his nightsuit and wiped his face clean of the black cosmetic.

He started the truck, pulling away from the litter of sprawled bodies and oily pools of blood spreading out across the tarmac in the moonlight like fattening spiders.

He wheeled around the nearest corner, driving fast with lights off, before any of the local police cars appeared this far into the maze of barracks.

He would make it.

The Executioner *had* to make it.

There was still Jack. . . .

20

Grimaldi, strapped to the stretcher attached to the frame of the chopper, wore a beatific smile of sedated unconsciousness, totally oblivious to everything happening around him.

Bolan turned from final inspection of his buddy's protective lacings. He gave the high sign to the pilot to prepare for lift-off.

The pilot in the cockpit of the helicopter increased the rotor speed. The engine overhead rumbled out of idle.

Bolan knelt at the door of the chopper for parting words with Karim.

The chopper had arrived at the refugee camp in their absence, a *mujahedeen* pilot risking his life to fly in medical supplies after receiving word that Aswadi's group had fallen under attack, exhausting their medical supplies.

The pilot offered to brave further risk by ferrying Bolan and Jack across the frontier battlefront into Iraq and hospitalization in time to save Jack's life.

Aswadi extended his hands.

The two men gripped in a firm two-handed affirmation of mutual respect.

"Live large, Karim. I've done all I can here."

"You gave us victory in the briefcase and files from the operation at Lavizan," Aswadi replied over the rumble of the chopper. "We now know the ones who have kept the presence of Khomeini alive to enslave our people long after the Ayatollah had returned to Satan."

"I'll watch the news," Bolan said, gripping the frame of the chopper for the lift-off. "They could say this is another false report of the old goat's death or maybe we'll hear now the Ayatollah suddenly passed away."

"The truth will destroy them," Aswadi asserted. "Mahmoud is dead, his conspiracy collapsed. The mechanism for propagating the myth of Khomeini's presence is finished. We are stronger than ever, thanks to you."

"Ah, one last thing, Karim. Keep a watch for our blond-haired lady."

"If she is CIA, she is the *mujahedeen*'s friend."

"I've got a feeling she's the one who called in this pilot after she got away from the camp tonight," said Bolan. "She'll be around to help you."

"She remains your enemy," Aswadi reminded him. "And yet Allah tells me you will encounter the woman again, Executioner. Your fates are destined to intertwine."

"Goodbye, Karim. Your people will win, tomorrow or soon. You fight the good fight. Stay hard."

And the chopper rose, banking away from the refugee camp, Karim Aswadi growing smaller beneath Bolan until the predawn dark swallowed man and camp.

The rotoring chopper slid gently into the desert sky.

Bolan braced himself against the inside of the open door. He sat there, letting the night wind feel good, cleansing away some of the thoughts from earlier, after he lost a blond beauty who somehow stayed with him like a dream you can't shake.

Maybe he would meet her again like Karim guessed, maybe not.

Bolan told himself he did not give a damn.

The Executioner had to make it alone on this last mile of Hellground Alley. It was Bolan's destiny.

He had been without the true love of a woman since April, and that fine woman would be alive today if she had not loved a soldier fated to War Everlasting.

Blood Alley could only be marched by a loner.

War Everlasting was this nightfighter's mistress, and Bolan would never be free of her.

He felt a sense of hard-earned satisfaction supplanting the weariness as he sat in the doorway of the chopper buzzing low beneath the radar grid across the desert.

They would make it in time for Jack.

And Bolan had faith in Aswadi, who represented the best Iran had to offer: strong, spiritual leadership for a ravaged land that could, would, be great again.

The Executioner had helped that along, a reward to gratify a fighting soldier who risked it all for the things that mattered.

And yeah, it had been nice knowing a nameless million-dollar blonde, however briefly, for the one warm human touch between man and woman to recharge, reaffirm for Mack Bolan the truth that some of the good things worth fighting for are very nice indeed.

For a man who lives large, the good fight would always be worth it.

MORE ADVENTURE
NEXT MONTH WITH

MACK BOLAN

#77 Hollywood Hell

The rootless and the ruthless

Each year thousands of teenage runaways are cast adrift in Hollywood. Lured by the lights of the city of illusion, many of these "chickens" wind up in porno flicks. And many of them wind up dead—as snuff-film victims.

This hit is personal as Mack Bolan sees his dead sister's face on every teenage vagrant in Tinsel Town. The Executioner is about to do some snuffing of his own. His target: the porn broker

DON PENDLETON'S EXECUTIONER
MACK BOLAN

Sergeant Mercy in Nam..The Executioner in the Mafia Wars...Colonel John Phoenix in the Terrorist Wars.... Now Mack Bolan fights his loneliest war! You've never read writing like this before. By fire and maneuver, Bolan will rack up hell in a world shock-tilted by terror. He wages unsanctioned war—everywhere!

GOLD EAGLE

Available wherever paperbacks are sold.

GET THE NEW WAR BOOK AND MACK BOLAN BUMPER STICKER <u>FREE!</u>

Mail this coupon today!

FREE! <u>THE NEW WAR BOOK</u> AND MACK BOLAN BUMPER STICKER
when you join our home subscription plan.

Gold Eagle Reader Service, a division of Worldwide Library
In U.S.A.: 2504 W. Southern Avenue, Tempe, Arizona 85282
In Canada: P.O. Box 2800, Postal Station A, 5170 Yonge Street, Willowdale, Ont. M2N 6J3

YES, rush me <u>The New War Book</u> and Mack Bolan bumper sticker FREE, and, under separate cover, my first six Gold Eagle novels. These first six books are mine to examine free for 10 days. If I am not entirely satisfied with these books, I will return them within 10 days and owe nothing. If I decide to keep these novels, I will pay just $1.95 per book (total $11.70). I will then receive the six Gold Eagle novels every other month, and will be billed the same low price of $11.70 per shipment. I understand that each shipment will contain two Mack Bolan novels, and one each from the Able Team, Phoenix Force, SOBs and Track libraries. There are no shipping and handling or any other hidden charges. I may cancel this arrangement at any time, and <u>The New War Book</u> and bumper sticker are mine to keep as gifts, even if I do not buy any additional books.

IMPORTANT BONUS: If I continue to be an active subscriber to Gold Eagle Reader Service, you will send me FREE, with every shipment, the AUTOMAG newsletter as a FREE BONUS!

Name _____ (please print) _____

Address _____ Apt. No. _____

City _____ State/Province _____ Zip/Postal Code _____

Signature _____ (If under 18, parent or guardian must sign.)

This offer limited to one order per household. We reserve the right to exercise discretion in granting membership. If price changes are necessary you will be notified.

116-BPM-PAE5

AA-SUB-1R